# MARRIED TO MY BOSS

LAURA BURTON

# COPYRIGHT

# PEYTON

My ankle boots are soaked and my socks are wet. It's been the wettest spring for *decades*, but not even the endless rain has been able to dull the mood in the city.

Rival business owners Zane Masters of *Got Cake?* and Elle Brook of *Elle's Kitchen* tied the knot a few months ago. It was a hot topic for weeks. This was after the most *ridiculous* proposal ever. The whole thing went viral online - the most popular upload has more than five million views. That's more views than the video of the mine shaft rescue in Columbia involving nineteen children. People are weird.

The crowd around me surges forward and carries me with it. But people aren't walking with their heads down and their hands in their pockets today. There's a lot of chatter. People are talking to one another in excited voices.

"I haven't been this excited since that billionaire hotel owner – David Marks, was it? – married his matchmaker."

"Emily James?"

"Yeah, her!"

The urge to roll my eyes at the conversation behind me is almost overwhelming. Don't get me wrong, I love a good fairy tale romance. And if some billionaire decides to sweep a woman off her feet, good for her!

I mean, I have a pile of letters back home to remind me that all my problems could go away if I got hit on by a billionaire.

But I'm a realist. Normal people like me do *not* get their happy ending by finding their one true love. I consider it a win if I make it to the end of the day without having to shout at the workmen outside my apartment for cat calling.

If I make it to the end of the month with enough money to buy some ice cream, I'm ecstatic.

A man to share said ice cream with would be a bonus. And he wouldn't even need to be rich.

Someone who can make me laugh and give a good foot rub. Is that too much to ask? Apparently, the fact that I'm thirty-three and still single doesn't help with channeling Miss Desirable. To make things worse, I've been stuck in the same dead-end job for years. I'm personal assistant to the editor-in-chief of a publishing house and I don't have the back-bone to ask for a raise.

Anyway, it's been three months since the Masters wedding at the Plaza hotel, catered by France Perrier, no less. And now there's a buzz in the air just outside the bakeries.

Looks like *Elle's Kitchen* is unveiling their new display. There's a huge crowd of photographers and curious people around the window. The scene looks a lot like something out of that 80's film - *The Mannequin*.

I shrug my jacket around me a little tighter, wipe the rain drops from my cheeks, and brace myself to walk through the crowd.

But just as I'm shouldering through, one of the bakery doors swings open and a revered silence falls. Elle Masters walks out.

I can't help staring. The unveiling must be happening right now. Zane Masters appears behind her and the two of them stand by the covered window like proud parents.

"Thank you all for coming to this special reveal," Elle calls out. Her hair is swept up in a loose bun. Perfect flyaway hairs frame her pretty face.

I can't see past her shoulders over the heads of the people, but I imagine she's wearing a designer dress that shows off her full figure and Zane has his arm around her waist. I have to strain my ears to catch the rest of the speech.

"This window is in honor of my mother, Elle Brook, and my grandmother at heart, Joyce Edwards. But it's not only for them. It's to remember the family we have loved and lost over the years. We always talk about grief like it's something to be ashamed of, or to hide from, but with our new angel cake, I want to show the world that grief can be beautiful. It can unite us. Life has many layers. So, I designed this cake with those layers, love, laughter, and loss." Elle takes a breath. I frown and crane to get a good look as she moves to the black curtain at the window.

"I present to you... the Angel Cake." She pulls the curtain back and cameras start to flash like crazy. "This treat is inspired by the angel cake that originated in England in the nineteenth century. There are three colored layers of sponge - pink for love, yellow for laughter, and white for loss. There's a decadent frosting to bind each layer and a dusting of powdered sugar on top. We hope you enjoy this cake as much as we do and that it reminds you to take time each day to appreciate all that life has to offer. Thank you."

Everyone moves forward to get a better look and I almost get jabbed in the stomach. Finally, there's a break in the crowd and I catch a glimpse of an elegant display of cakes on a small dinner table in the window. Smiling women beam out at me from framed photos, and there's a delicate gold locket lying on one of the plates.

I move away from the crowd as soon as I've got a good look. The theme is surprisingly deep for a cake shop. A part of me is impressed. I've suffered a loss too, but what do people say about the ones they did *not* love?

I'm jolted out of my thoughts when my

phone buzzes, and I answer the call on autopilot. "Yes, Mr. Rockwood."

I didn't even need to look at the caller ID to know it was my boss.

"I need to see you immediately," he says.

"Now? I was just on my way home-" I begin to say. There's no use, though. I know what his answer is.

"Now."

Grumbling to myself, I call a cab and do my best to dry off my boots with a tissue. I do a quick makeup fix on the ride back to the office.

Mr. Rockwood does not like to wait. The urgency in his voice made it clear he's already in a bad mood.

It's the perfect way to end an already terrible day.

I burst into his office. "Yes, Mr. Rockwood. You wanted me?"

The leather armchair facing the ceiling-to-floor length windows swivels around and my boss appears. He rests his elbows on his desk and his gray eyes travel north and south as he takes in my soggy appearance. I cross my arms to conceal the damp patches on my blouse.

"What happened to you? You look like you just climbed out of the Hudson."

I grit my teeth. The question is rhetorical. An answer will only irritate him.

"Sorry, Mr. Rockwood. What do you need?" I pull out my phone and open the Notes app, ready for his list of demands.

"You," he says. His voice is curt, and my thumb hovers over my phone as my brain tries to process the word.

"Me?" He gestures to the leather seat in front of his desk. "Please, take a seat, P…"

"Peyton," I remind him.

*Really?* I've been here almost a decade now, and this man still doesn't remember my name.

"Peyton," he says, smiling now.

The man is as stiff as a board. I can't help noticing the strain in his neck as he frowns and shuffles through a stack of papers.

"Tell me about yourself, Peyton. Where are you from?"

My mouth forms an o, but I shut it quickly. I have no idea where Mr. Rockwood is going with this, but the wicked glint in his eye is a tell. He's cooking up something and I'm 100% sure I'm going to hate it.

"I was raised in New Jersey, sir. Then I moved to New York for this job. I've lived here ever since." It's a half-truth, the real reason I left New Jersey was because my foster parents died and I needed a fresh start.

The thought of them hits me like a punch to the gut. Mr. Rockwood doesn't seem to notice.

"Excellent. So, you're American, yes?"

"Yes... What is this—"

"I'll cut to the chase with you, Peyton," Mr. Rockwood says abruptly. He leans forward and gives me one of his *I mean business* stares. That look is usually reserved for difficult clients. "I have a contract here for you to sign. If you're willing to accept the terms, I shall pay you handsomely."

My ears prick up at the mention of payment. "Are you offering me a promotion?" I ask. My heart starts to race as I take the contract from his hand. "Well, it's more of a favor... Strictly professional, of course."

I start reading the contract and my face twists in confusion. "You want me to *marry* you?"

I look at him quizzically. "I need you to be

my wife for one year," he explains. "When the year is up, I'll pay you fifty thousand dollars."

I almost choke on my own saliva as I splutter. "What?"

Mr. Rockwood peels off his designer jacket and rises from his seat. He moves to the table at the corner of the room. "Can I fix you a drink?" He holds up a crystal cut glass. I shake my head. The last thing I need right now is alcohol in my system.

I take another look at the contract to check he's not kidding. My eyes stretch wide at the zeroes on the page. "But *why*? And why me?"

Mr. Rockwood downs a drink and smacks his lips together with a sigh. "As you know, I'm from England. I may have failed to take the immigration process seriously. I'll save you the unsavory details. The bottom line is, if I want to stay here and keep my job, I need a wife. An *American* wife." He raises his empty glass to me. "That's you." Then he turns to look out the windows; a tall man with a stiff back. "The immigration office needs evidence to show that this marriage is authentic, which is why I need you to sign up for a year."

I gulp. "Are you asking me to commit fraud?"

Mr. Rockwood turns to look at me and his gaze is so stern, I hold my breath. "Tell me, what would you do with the money?"

I bite my lip and think about it. If someone offered me one hundred dollars right now, I'd feel like a millionaire. With fifty thousand I could quit my job (and I would have to, after being married to my boss), rent a nice house in the suburbs... Maybe even start my own fashion line.

Mr. Rockwood is suddenly close enough to plant his hand on the back of my chair. "Can you do this for me?" he asks.

I swallow. "A year of my life... That's a long time. What if I have a boyfriend and he proposes to me next week?"

Mr. Rockwood's smile fades and he turns serious as he seems to consider this. "*Do* you have a boyfriend?"

My eyes sting with humiliation. "No."

Mr. Rockwood's face turns gleeful again. "You're playing a hard bargain. Fifty thousand dollars is a lot of money, you know."

"And a year of my life in my thirties is a lot to take," I shoot back. My mouth seems to be working on its own now. I usually keep my sassy comebacks in my head.

"Fine. One hundred thousand dollars."

"No," I say, shaking my head. "I'm not lying to the immigration office."

"*Five* hundred thousand dollars. Come on, Peyton." Mr. Rockwood and I are suddenly in an intense staring contest. Then he makes another offer without batting an eyelid. "One million dollars."

I gasp. "Surely, with that kind of money you can just buy yourself a visa. You know, by investing the money in a business."

Mr. Rockwood bristles and something flashes behind his eyes.

What is he hiding?

"What do you say, Peyton? Can you bear to be married to me for one year in exchange for a million dollars? The offer is on the table, but it won't be there for long."

"I need to think about it…"

"Three…" he cuts in.

I lift a brow. "Are you counting down?"

"I need to know *now*, Peyton. I have more at stake here than you know. Two…"

I study his face with narrowed eyes. My common sense is yelling at me to run out the door. "One," he says, and his eyes bore into the depths of my soul.

One million dollars will change my life. I shut my eyes and suck in a breath. "Fine. I'll do it."

# SEBASTIAN

*Financial risks aside,* there are a number of reasons why I shouldn't marry my personal assistant.

I'm honestly not concerned about the financials because she did sign the pre-nup.

When the marriage comes to its inevitable end, at least she can't come after me for more money.

I don't expect that Peyton would do anything like that, though. She's never asked for so much as an extra dime in years.

It's part of what makes her perfect for the position of my pretend wife.

I need someone to play the role, answer all

of the questions correctly, and keep quiet. There's no better candidate than my shy, submissive PA who knows just about everything there is to know about me.

She knows how I like my coffee - black with two sugars.

She has a sixth sense about my mood. She knows the precise time to interrupt a meeting and bring it to an end with a fake emergency.

She knows that I'm allergic to two things: Aspirin and authors with big egos.

And yet, expecting her to masquerade as my wife for a whole year can't be fair on anyone, let alone Peyton.

Did I expect her to take the first offer? No. But I like to drive a hard bargain, even if I know what I'm asking is both unconventional and maybe a bit unethical... Actually, it's completely unethical.

And when my accountant hears about this, he'll have a lecture or two to deliver. The guy is as straight as a banana, he won't be lecturing me about the risk of a ruined reputation. He'll be more concerned about the number of zeroes I've promised Ms. Bishop.

But what is a million dollars in the grand scheme of things?

With her help, I'll have access to billions of dollars.

Not that I'll be letting her in on *that* secret.

Sure, she's not the gold-digging type now, but if she finds out I'm hoping to inherit a multi-billion-pound estate from my grandpa, that might change. After all, they say money changes people.

I can't afford any risk of her not going through with the divorce.

Which is why I need her to believe this is just a deal for a visa to live in the States permanently.

I go over all of the reasons why this isn't a terrible idea one more time, but I know no amount of deep thinking can ease the tension in my stomach.

At the bottom of my mental pro/con list are three simple facts.

1. I need this.
2. Peyton needs money.
3. It's a win-win, and when this is all over, we'll go our separate ways and live our best lives.

I'm certain that in two years' time, we'll

look back on this whole thing and laugh. Maybe even feel a sense of gratitude.

It's dark and raining when I leave the office. Again.

Summer feels like a lifetime ago, and it certainly doesn't feel like spring with all of the terrible weather we've been having.

The smell of wet grass and the sound of wheels splashing into puddles remind me of home.

And by home, I mean England.

I grew up in the country, just outside of Reading. It was a great place to be a teenager. A train ride from London, and a cycle into the city, where just about every form of entertainment was available.

From all-you-can-eat pizza buffets and arcades, to skateboard parks and nature trails. There was never a dull day.

Except for the days in school, listening to my history professor talking about the Tudors in a mind-numbing drone. Falling asleep during Mr. Marlow's lectures was a given.

Boarding school set me up for college life. I went on to Cambridge University, and while the other kids were out partying until sunrise or crying over being away from their parents for the first time; I was managing my days perfectly.

I've always been independent. A lone wolf, with very few people that I trust. And I like it that way. But my old-fashioned Grandpa put that ridiculous marriage clause in his will. Now I'll have to get out of my comfort zone.

Grandpa was an inventor. I have memories of summers at his bungalow. He turned his garage into a workshop and spent most of his time in there, fixing things, taking them apart, creating new things. I stood for hours in his garage, enthralled, watching him work.

My Grandma was at least four inches taller than him, and that came with a few problems. But they were problems my grandpa took great delight in solving. He fitted new kitchen cabinets and fixed them higher up so she wouldn't need to stoop over the counter when she was chopping onions.

He installed new mirrors, because the old ones didn't show the top half of her face. He even made a height-adjusting bed. It looked like a mahogany sleigh bed, but with the simple tap of a button, it would rise up a few inches, or go back down.

My Grandma was beautiful. She always had her hair pinned up and her lips painted red. She might have been a model in her day, but we never spoke about that.

She never talked about her past. And as a young, ignorant man, I never thought to ask. It's something I regret bitterly now. After she passed away, her name was like a poison. My grandpa's face would pale whenever her name came up in conversation, and he'd make excuses to leave the room. I never had the opportunity to ask him about her, either.

I have only one stark memory of something she told me. She said her life before she married my grandfather was like "living in black and white." And when she fell in love, she "started to see the world in technicolor."

Grandma spoke in riddles at the best of times. It made her mysterious. She always smelled of peppermint. Now, whenever I catch a whiff of that scent, her face floods my mind and I remember happier, simpler times.

Sometimes, I suspect Grandpa started to see the world in black and white after she died.

His quirks became more and more pronounced after her death. He started talking to himself, muttering under his breath. And his face wrinkled up like he'd been soaking in the bath for too long.

He never shed a single tear in front of me, thanks to the stiff upper lip us Brits are raised to have, but I suspect all the extra wrinkles were due to many nights weeping in the dark.

That was when he dug deep and focused completely on inventing.

One of his many inventions was a mechanism designed to make a garage roof move up and down. Another was a cabinet with a hidden panel to hide important documents, and his most famous invention was the reflector now used to line roads.

Rumor has it he earned £1 for every reflector on all the roads in England. But that's not true.

He got £1 for every reflector installed on all the roads in every country around the world.

I'm not sure of his total worth. All I know is it's a lot.

To the average person, my grandpa was a simple man. He never moved out of that small, two-bed bungalow in Surrey. When I asked him why, he said he couldn't leave the home he'd lived in with my Grandma and raised my mother in.

Even though he had the money to fix any problem, he still insisted on working hard and being frugal. I'll hazard a guess that even he had no idea how much he really had in the bank.

I, too, appreciate hard work. I guess it's something he passed down to me.

I'm the first at the office in the morning and the last to leave.

As the old saying goes, a business cannot outgrow its CEO. And as Editor-in-Chief of my own publishing company, I make it my mission to set the example. But my personal life has suffered because of it.

I don't have friends. Only sycophants who like to say we're friends. They're only around while they're benefitting from me in some way. I don't even have a dog, let alone a wife.

There's never been any time to date.

Getting married and having my own family simply hasn't been on my list of priorities.

My mom died two years ago, and my dad

remarried and moved to Australia. I just focused more on my work.

Now I'm the sole heir to my grandfather's fortune, a man on the precipice of monumental change. With this money, I can reduce my work hours and focus on what I want to do with the rest of my life - focus on the legacy I want to leave behind.

The thing is, I've become a slave to work. Life is exactly as Grandma put it - black and white. I'm missing something big, and I can't put my finger on what.

New York is where I'll put down my roots, grow my name and build a more fulfilling life. Maybe I'll adopt a rescue, like a lazy, golden retriever to snooze in front of the fire.

That dream was so close to becoming a reality when my grandpa's probate was in process. I had no idea he would throw a spanner in the works.

The will reading feels, simultaneously, like a millennium and a second ago. The tiny office had a woody smell to it, and the oversized gentleman panted as he sat at the desk to pore over the paperwork.

"Your grandfather bequeaths his entire

fortune, property, and all of his assets to you. But has directed that it be in holding until you celebrate your first wedding anniversary."

I nearly choked on my coffee. "Excuse me?"

The corner of his mouth lifted briefly and his black beady eyes settled on mine. I sensed he was making a concerted effort to be professional, but the sympathy in his gaze was unmistakable. "It is a rather unconventional request, indeed. He wrote this for you." He handed me a letter, and the envelope looked far too new to suggest he wrote it a long time ago.

"When did he write this?" I asked.

The man's bushy brows lifted. "It's dated the first day of January, this year."

I gritted my teeth. That was the last time I had seen him. I thought back to the things I said that day, and my blood turned cold.

I didn't ask any other questions, and I still haven't opened the letter.

The fact is, I'm not interested in what it has to say. It won't change anything. He's gone and so is any opportunity to talk this over with him.

And no matter what's said in the blasted

letter that now haunts me from my nightstand, I'll need to have been married for a year to access my inheritance. Every day counts.

With that thought, I let myself into my Manhattan home, throw my bag on the couch and pull my phone out of my pocket to make a call.

"Peyton, pack your bags, I'm picking you up early in the morning."

"Where are we going?" Her voice is faint and laced with shock. I'm almost concerned about how fast this is happening. Almost.

The sooner we start the clock, the sooner this façade can end. I need this to happen quickly, and if I'm to keep up with the lie I told about the immigration office, I need to be creative.

I smirk, wondering why she even needs to ask the question.

"Where do you think a couple can have a spontaneous wedding that won't look suspicious to the immigration office?"

She's silent for a few moments and I can picture her dark, narrow brows furrow while she thinks. It's the look she gives me when I ask her if my tie is crooked.

"Are you telling me we're going to Vegas?"

There's a hint of anticipation in her voice now. My smirk widens.

# PEYTON

*I*'m still shaking when I get back to my apartment, and it's not my soaked clothes giving me a chill. It's the stark realization that I've signed a contract to be married to my boss.

Mr. Rockwood. The moodiest guy on the planet.

A man so cocky and self-important that I don't even know his first name.

No one knows his first name. All his mail is addressed to Mr. Rockwood.

And soon, I'm going to be *Mrs.* Rockwood.

Am I crazy? Have I *actually* lost my mind?

My hands won't stop trembling, so I head

for the bathroom to fill up the tub with hot water. Times like these call for a bubble bath and scented candles.

As the water gushes out, I strike a match and try to decide which candle to light.

Does the future Mrs. Rockwood relax to the scent of arctic breeze? Or cotton candy?

I light the cotton candy one before the flame reaches my fingers and blow the match out with a weak breath. Then I shrug off my damp jacket and start unbuttoning my shirt.

"I'm crazy!" I cry out.

"Crazy! Crazy!" squawks the parrot from the other room. I clamp my teeth together and will my mouth to stay shut, so I don't give the bird anything else to repeat a million times.

My heart is galloping like a spooked horse.

We're going to Vegas in the morning!

I slip into the bath and let the water rise up to my chin.

The warmth of the fragrant water settles my nerves just enough for me to let out a long, deep breath.

*Okay, Peyton. Let's think about this logically.*

I've signed a year of my life into a marriage with my boss. To convince the immigration office that our relationship is legit, I need to move into his place, take his name, and act like I'm totally in love with the biggest jerk I know.

Piece of cake, right?

I hold my breath and sink below the surface of the water. The warmth takes over my face.

*What have I done?*

This is where a concerned bestie would come in with all sorts of questions. Or a wise aunt would share some warnings.

But I have no one. The only soul that has anything to say to me is Larry. Larry is still squawking "crazy, crazy," like a broken record.

But Larry is right. I *am* crazy.

Who signs a contract to marry someone they can't stand? Who agrees to lie to immigration officers, and commit all kinds of felonies in the process, just for a check with a bunch of zeros on it?

I can hardly stand being in the same room as Mr. Rockwood during work hours. Now I'll have to share his house and break bread with the guy every night for the next one year.

It's madness.

*But just think what you'd do with a million dollars!*

I'll pay off my student loan and all my credit cards. I can move to another state. I could literally wipe the slate clean and do whatever I want.

No more kissing up to my boss when we're done with this. Or worrying about what mood he's going to be in when I get into the office. No more long hours with unfair pay.

No more debts. No more instant noodles.

Visualizing my future happy self brings me out of my panic, and an entirely new sensation takes hold. The only thing I can do now is get through this.

My mind moves to the pressing matter: I need to pack.

Mr. Rockwood is picking me up in the morning.

Why does that statement make my stomach flip?

I jerk myself out of the water and cough, wiping bubbles from my eyes.

I've never been to Vegas before.

I've always pictured shiny casinos, fabulously dressed showpeople walking the streets, and fantastic music blasting out of speakers twenty-four hours a day.

I wonder how long we'll be staying. Mr. Rockwood told me to pack a bag, so I guess it's not a day trip.

I know he's a workaholic - the man has not taken a vacation day outside of the holiday season in the decade that I've worked for him - so we'll probably be gone for the weekend.

My stomach does another flip.

I shouldn't be excited about this.

It's not like we'll be having any fun. Mr. Rockwood is so serious and brooding. The guy has a permanent line between his brows from all the deep thinking he does. And I've never seen him wear anything but a suit.

Going to the entertainment capital of the world can't be much fun with a partner who's about as enjoyable to be around as an angry houseplant.

Like a cactus.

My mind flashes back to the contract and the scene plays out like a mini movie in front of me.

Mr. Rockwood strode across his office with a grim face and squared shoulders.

"Let me go through the particulars…" he said, swirling his drink. "You are contracted to be legally married to me. However, you are not required to consummate the marriage."

I gulped. He said it like the activity would somehow not involve him. And so plainly too. He met my shocked gaze with a hard look, completely unabashed.

It took a second, but I recovered myself. "That's a relief."

"You will reside with me from the moment we are married, but I will make provisions for you to have your own room and wing of the house."

My jaw dropped. "Wing?" I asked. What does he live in, a castle?

He ignored my question and continued his pacing. The familiar scent of his sandalwood cologne washed over me. "We may be required to display affection and intimacy at public events and at the immigration office."

I listened to him list the rest of the rules.

But my brain was caught up on one word.

"Intimacy?" I blurted.

He stopped and looked at me again. "Hand holding. Touching. Chaste kisses."

"*Chaste* kisses?" I repeated, trying and

failing to hide the amusement in my voice. I shouldn't have bothered. My humor was lost on him. Mr. Rockwood didn't even glance in my direction as he carried on his train of thought.

I towel off and flop on my bed with a sigh as I try to imagine Mr. Rockwood pretending to be my husband.

Holding hands? I don't see it happening.

He flinches when I brush his shoulder in passing, or when our fingers graze as I pass him a cup of coffee. How is he going to tolerate touching me?

A huge part of me is skeptical about this whole thing. How are we going to make this work?

And speaking of work... What are we going to say to the others in the office when we show up married?

Larry has shut up now, much to my relief. I lay in darkness, waiting for my hair to air dry and wondering what clothes to pack.

What do you wear to a fake-real wedding in Vegas?

Do I pack flats or heels?

The thought makes me laugh. Why do I even need to wonder what to pack? The only things in my closet that aren't work clothes are a denim dress I haven't worn since 2010, a red Ted Baker dress I got at an outlet last year, and a million oversized t-shirts.

I'm gonna have to take it all with me and figure it out. I thought personal preparedness was about keeping tinned food and lentils in the pantry, and a backpack full of survival gear.

No one told me a pretend wedding could be a thing.

If I had known about the "get married to my boss in Vegas" emergency, I'd have at least bought a couple of cute things from Target to keep on standby.

The loud music from the apartment above mine pulls me back into the moment and reminds me I have things to do. Now is not the time to overthink.

I get into my night shirt and scramble around my dark room, stuffing whatever I can into my gym bag - yes, gym bag. I don't go on vacations, so it's the only thing I own to store my clothes in.

I probably look like a burglar to anyone looking into my bedroom window right now, stumbling around in the dark and stuffing things into a black duffle bag. But I'm worried that as soon as I turn on a light, all of this will feel too real and I'll have a panic attack. Besides, Larry will see me and start chirping "crazy, crazy," again.

The bird must be able to read my mind. His voice trails into my room.

"Alexa, all lights on."

My entire apartment is suddenly flooded with light.

*That sneaky parrot! Why does he have to be so dang clever?*

Sighing, I walk into the living room. My green feathered friend has his head cocked to the side and a smug look on his face. He's clearly proud of himself. Using my Alexa is his new favorite trick. I guess after hearing me say it every night for the past couple of years, he finally picked it up.

I give him his feed, lift up his cage and cross the hall to Apartment 2b. Joan tells me she's happy to watch him while I'm gone.

A few minutes later, I'm back in my empty apartment.

The jitters are back as I look wistfully

around my place. After tonight, I'll be married.

This is my last night in my own home. Who knows when I'll be back for good?

Something tells me it's gonna be a long night and I'm not gonna sleep a wink.

# SEBASTIAN

I park outside a block of tired-looking apartments in a side of town I'd never usually drive down. The few trees planted in the sidewalk are bare. There's a beaten-up couch on the side of the street, surrounded by trash bags, and I imagine the residents often hear cats screeching in alleyways during the night.

I double-check and triple-check the address.

This cannot be where Peyton lives. How does she get in and out of her apartment unscathed? If the wild cats don't get her, the uneven steps leading to her door look slick with grease - an accident waiting to happen.

Has she not seen Home Alone?

I turn off the ignition and climb out of the car, narrowly avoiding a puddle. The air smells damp and musty - like a pile of wet clothes left in the washing machine for too long.

I nod to the old lady who passes me on my way to the door. Instead of acknowledging my existence, she mutters to herself as though deep in conversation with someone.

I take care to not lose footing on the steps and rap on the door to the apartment. The white, peeling paint stares back at me, threatening. I half-expect it to give me lead poisoning if I knock again.

That's when I notice the rusty box on the side, with a line of buttons. One of them is labeled; *2a-Peyton Bishop.*

I press the button, prompting a buzz. A familiar voice calls out from the speaker. "Yes?"

"It's Mr. Rockwood, here to collect—"

There's a bang so loud it almost blasts my eardrums, then static.

"Hello?" I ask, hesitant. I eye the brass handle and wonder if I can shoulder my way in. A succession of panicked thoughts takes over my mind.

What if Peyton tripped on a rogue wire?

What if her intercom is as suspicious as the one on the outside?

Maybe she got electrocuted and is now passed out on the floor requiring medical attention?

I'm just about to press down on the handle when Peyton's breathless voice comes back.

"Sorry. I'll be right down."

The intercom squeals before it cuts off again, and I wait for the front door to open.

I'm trying to work out why my stomach is knotted. A sense of foreboding takes over me. It doesn't make sense to feel this way. This plan was my idea after all.

And who better to do this with than the person I spend eight hours a day with each week?

Peyton doesn't make me nervous. Not usually.

In fact, she's the one to calm me when I'm tense.

Today, though, my stomach is doing flips and I can't tell you what that's about.

The door opens and Peyton's flushed face

floods my view. Then a brisk wind blows her hair back, and for a few seconds, everything seems to happen in slow motion.

Her thick lashes flutter, and her lips curve upward as she steps out through the front with a beaten-up gym bag hanging off her. My mind registers several details before the door slams shut behind her and everything speeds up again.

She loses balance, probably from the deathly combination of a slippery step and her gym bag. But I was half expecting this type of scenario to play out.

My right arm moves of its own accord and the next thing I know, her body is pressed up on mine and I'm clutching her waist.

Her face is mere inches from mine; I can feel her minty breath tickling my upper lip. Her lashes flutter again as she stares at me in shock.

"Are you all right?" I ask, still clutching her like a porcelain doll.

This woman is worth billions of dollars.

She stiffens against me and I get the message. We step away from each other when I loosen my grip on her. "I'm fine," she says. My jaw tenses as I search her eyes. "How dare you be so careless?" As soon as the words come out of my mouth, I know I'm being a lot harsher than I need to be. But I can't stop now. "You could have fallen down these steps, and hurt yourself!" I conclude lamely. Peyton's brows shoot up and her eyes grow dull as she turns to walk to the pavement. I reluctantly let her go.

The air is awkward between us now, and I swallow against the dryness in my throat.

"May I take your bag?" I offer. But the question triggers movement in Peyton's brows again. She frowns at me with suspicion.

"No, I've got it," she says slowly.

I sigh. Barking at her isn't likely to help breed trust between us. I need to get my mouth in check. And my hands too, apparently. Because they're itching to hold her again.

She sees me as her boss. Nothing more. And after that outburst, she must think that I still regard her as a mere employee. Our marriage is just an extension of her current job description.

Of course, she doesn't know how acutely I'm aware of what she's worth to me. It's like being in possession of a rare jewel. I'll do anything to keep her from harm.

The awkward silence continues on the drive to the airport. I keep my eyes on the road, painfully aware of Peyton next to me.

I can't remember the last time a woman sat in my car. In fact, I'm fairly certain it's never happened before.

She's placed a hand on the center console and she's so close, I can feel her body heat on my arm. It's setting my hairs on end. I swallow hard and clear my throat.

Why does she make me so nervous now?

Maybe it's because there is so much at stake. But if I don't stop thinking about it, I might just end up having a heart attack and not make it to my first wedding anniversary.

I push a button and Chopin starts blasting out of the speakers. Classical music never fails to settle my nerves. The music washes over me and I let my shoulders drop.

Then I catch a look from Peyton; her brow is cocked. I've never met a woman with such animated facial features in my life. But then her expression turns neutral, as though she caught herself.

"What?" I ask.

Peyton shakes her head and her long hair swooshes. "Nothing. I just never pegged you for a guy who'd love the classics."

Now it's my turn to lift a brow. "And what kind of music did you expect me to like?"

Peyton shrugs. "I don't know… Something aggressive."

The comment nips my insides and I frown. Do I come across as aggressive?

That's not how I see myself at all.

I like to command respect, sure. I have a backbone and won't let anyone bully me. Maybe I'm overworked from time to time.

Stressed, even.

But *aggressive?*

The word troubles me as I drive on in silence. I'd rather not ask Peyton to elaborate, though. She might have some other blunt descriptions I don't want to hear.

I can handle a literary agent shouting abuse to my face. I can have hard conversations with employees who have been slacking, and take the snide comments they whisper as I walk by.

But Peyton is different. She's always been on my side and had my back. For ten years, she's done everything I've asked of her, and more.

She's there to jump in with a latte or a friendly smile when I'm having a bad day.

She's the one person in my life who doesn't talk back or look at me with contempt.

I'm not sure I can handle the idea of Peyton's criticism.

"Sorry," she says, sensing the shift in my mood. "I don't know where that came from. It's not that I think you're aggressive."

She's lying, but I appreciate it.

When we pull into the airport parking lot, I steal a glance in Peyton's direction. "If we're to convince anyone that our marriage is real, we need to know everything about each other. And it looks like we have a lot of work to do."

"You're right." Peyton laughs. "I don't even know your first name."

I turn off the ignition and search her face, wondering if she is joking. She's not.

Now that I think about it. I've never told anyone my name.

Why?

Because nobody ever asked.

It's a stark reminder of the fact that I've had walls up ever since I moved to the States.

I've been so engrossed in my mission to build my business and reputation that I forgot to let people in.

I have to shake my head to clear it. Peyton is looking at me expectantly. "We're going to be taking our vows," I say. "So, I suppose you should know…"

Peyton's face lights up with anticipation and her eyes twinkle. I try to ignore the funny feeling in my stomach that sight triggers. I clear my throat instead of smiling back like a fool.

"My name is Sebastian."

# PEYTON

*W*hat's in a name?

Working in a publishing house for the past decade has taught me that words have power, and not all words are equal.

If I'm reading about a man professing his undying love for the heroine, the tone of the scene depends on the words.

If an author uses terms of endearment like, "darling, dearest, love of my life," it's sweet and gentle. But the entire mood shifts if the words "babe" or "baby" come into play.

I've also learned that not all names are equal. There's a marked difference between John and Jonathan, for example. The former is somewhat casual. It casts a mental image of an astute, stubborn, but loyal man who likes to wear polo shirts. 'Jonathan' transforms the man into a more boyish character, one with a friendly disposition but too much gel in his hair.

Those are my interpretations. But names conjure up all kinds of memories, feelings, and images to different people. Which is what fascinates me about the written word.

A thousand readers can experience the same book in a thousand different ways. There is so much work in what readers do. They take simple words from a page and paint an elaborate set of moving pictures and sounds in their head, bringing the author's writing to life in the most transcen-dent way.

When Sebastian told me his name, it hit me somewhere in the chest, and a rush of tingles scattered through my whole body. I don't understand why.

It's just another word, after all. It shouldn't cause any kind of monumental reaction.

But my body missed the memo.

My gut squeezed and I gasped like a maiden swooning in a pirate movie.

*Sebastian Rockwood. All these years, and I never knew his name.*

Now that I do, it's unlocked something inside of me and set off some sort of chain reaction. Maybe it's the thrill of knowing something intimate about the man. That, combined with the certainty that I'm now the only one at the office who knows it?

Whatever the reason, my boss's sex appeal just ramped up several notches. His name is running on repeat in my head.

I can't figure out why. But it doesn't help that he's been looking at me in this cheeky yet vulnerable way It kind of makes me want to do something rash.

Something like squeal and punch the air with triumph.

Or tell him one of my darkest secrets.

Or maybe, just maybe, something even more daring and crazy.

Like marry him.

I almost laugh out loud. Because we're doing that already.

"Sebastian," I say, trying the name aloud.

I love the way it rolls off my tongue. Sebastian's eyes flash and his smile widens. He likes the way it sounds, too.

"It'll be our little secret," he says, grinning now.

*Is he flirting with me?*

This guy snapped at me in front of my own apartment, and was moody the entire ride to the airport. Now he's behaving like he's a cocky quarterback talking to one of the cheerleaders under the bleachers.

I snort. "As if we need any more secrets."

At least this one isn't about breaking the law.

Every time I hear his name in my mind, a rush of tingles spreads through my body.

*Sebastian. Sebastian. Sebastian!*

I twist my fingers in a lock of my hair and chew my lip.

His name is sending all sorts of inappropriate images across my mind's eye.

Like breathing out his name in bed.

My hand flies to my mouth as though my body is trying to stop the thoughts from coming out. Sebastian is still looking at me in amusement.

"What's wrong? Your cheeks are pink."

"Nothing. I'm hot." I avert my eyes and start fanning myself, but I can still feel his gaze on me and it burns.

What has gotten into me? This is Mr. Rockwood. Moody Mr. Rockwood who never tells a joke or cracks a smile, not even when I do.

I meet his amused gaze for the briefest moment, then look away again, grinning to myself.

"Yes. You are hot," he says, and now I've got butterflies. "But that's no reason to blush."

Then Sebastian does something I don't think I've ever seen him do.

He laughs.

The deep rumble lights up several parts of my body and I hold my breath.

What is wrong with me? I'm giddy like a high school girl sitting next to her crush and I haven't even had my morning coffee. Maybe my blood sugar is dipping and it's making me jittery.

Yes. That must be it. Because there's no way my boss is turning me into a giggly fan girl.

"Shall we go?"

It's not a question. Sebastian climbs out of the car and I follow him. He goes to the trunk for our bags and I lean against the Mercedes with my eyes shut so I can take yoga breaths.

Slowly, the practical and very sensible side of my brain kicks in with some grounding thoughts.

This is my grumpy, insufferable boss.

Nothing has changed here.

He's only being nice because he needs me.

*All of this is fake. An act. Don't fall for it, Peyton.*

In fact, he's probably just starting the act now in case the immigration office gets security footage of the parking lot.

Yes. This is all for the ruse.

Soon enough, Sebastian will be back to his old, cold ways.

The trunk closes with a thump and I jump, blinking away an image of the cold Sebastian I've always known.

He walks over with my gym bag in one hand and a designer luggage case in the other. His face is sunnier than a summer's day. When he reaches my side, he locks the car with his clicker and actually winks at me.

Winks!

*What a notion!* as Mrs. Bennett would say.

Sebastian offers me his arm and I resist the urge to scan the deserted parking lot for cameras. I guess the show has already begun.

One million dollars, I remind myself.

Then I link my arm with his and squeeze his bicep. It tenses under me, and it's much more muscular than I anticipated. I beam at him. "Vegas, here we come."

# SEBASTIAN

*V*egas is hot.

The second we walk out of the airport, hot air fills my lungs and it's like walking into a furnace. Golden sunshine beats down on us, and within seconds, I've broken out into a sweat.

Peyton's dainty hand is resting on the crook of my arm and I haven't decided how I feel about her touch.

The odd thing is it feels normal. But in the past, even the briefest touch could send an unsettling zap through me.

There's no time to think about it, though. There are matters far more pressing to focus my attention on. Matters like our upcoming nuptials.

"We'll take our bags to our suite, then head out later. I've booked the chapel for this afternoon," I say, helping Peyton into a cab. She slides across the back seat and eyes me with a nervous smile as she buckles her seatbelt. "You're not hanging around, are you?"

I stiffen. "The sooner we do this, the sooner it's over."

Peyton's smile vanishes. "Right. Of course."

We settle into silence, looking out our windows as the cab crawls along the Las Vegas strip.

Tall casinos tower over us in elaborate displays of all shapes and colors. "Is that the Eiffel Tower?" Peyton says in a breathy voice, pointing. "And the statue of Liberty! How cute. It's so small!"

She's adorable. My cheeks pinch as I listen to her marvel at all the monuments. But when she turns to me, I force a neutral expression.

"Do you think we have time to ride a gondola?"

It's the last thing I expect her to ask, and the hopeful tone in her voice takes me aback.

But I clear my throat and give her a stern expression. "This is not a vacation, Peyton."

Her eyes go dull, but she nods. "Of course, sorry."

I look out of my window again. A stream of tourists walks by to the soundtrack of some upbeat music that's been muted by the car windows. Peyton breaks the silence. "I can't stop thinking about the immigration interviews. Our story needs to be convincing..." She bites her lip and looks at me. "Does it come across as believable that we simply went to Vegas and got married, even though we'd not been seen dating at all?"

"Fine," I say, gritting my teeth. She looks at me, her pale hands resting on her faded denim jeans. "We can look around the Casinos before we head to the chapel."

Peyton's face brightens. "Sounds like fun."

*W*ith just a couple of hours to our nuptials, I take Peyton on an express tour of the strip. We grab a couple of drinks, and Peyton clutches her oversized cup as we walk through the expansive casinos, taking in the displays.

"The immigration office could ask for the security camera footage from any of these places," whispers Peyton, her eyes looking around for them. I nod. Then I make sure to touch Peyton like she's my real fiancée.

By the time we have a couple of drinks in us, our defenses are down and Peyton doesn't react when I rest my hand on the small of her back at the roulette table.

When we marvel at the fountain show outside the Bellagio, Peyton's arm snakes across my back and she grabs my waist, then puts her head on my shoulder.

I'm surprised how nicely she fits against my body. I look around at the throng of couples standing nearby and they're all standing like us. Hip to hip, arms wrapped around each other. To them, I'm certain that Peyton and I look like just another couple. If I was sober, this would be very weird and awkward for both of us. Especially Peyton, who looked at me with repulsion when I offered to help her back at her apartment.

By the time we reach the Chapel of the Bells, there's alcohol pumping through our veins and Peyton is giggling. I don't think I've ever heard her giggle. It's an alien sound, but not one that I hate. In fact, in my intoxicated state, everything about Peyton is like taking another shot. I don't hold back my grin as we walk through the doors. I clutch Peyton's tiny sides and walk in behind her.

"Sebastian Rockwood and Peyton Bishop. We have an appointment at four-thirty," I say to the woman at the desk.

The next hour passes in a blur of laughter, cheesy 80's music, and flamboyant actors cracking jokes. Peyton bumps her mouth against mine and breaks into a fit of giggles while I settle the bill.

We leave the chapel laughing, arm in arm, and head for the nearest bar.

We spend the rest of the evening drinking far too much and staggering up and down the strip.

"Look at that star, Sebastian," Peyton says. I follow her line of sight.

"That's not a star, it's the Strat."

Peyton halts and wobbles on the spot. I brace her with my hands, though my head is starting to spin too. Then we both look up at the huge tower with a bright, beaming light at its top.

"Why can I hear screams?" Peyton asks, her brows pinching together.

I point upward. "See that mechanical arm at the top? People are on that."

Peyton gasps. "It's a ride? It's hanging over the edge!"

We stand together, listening to the faint screams coming from above our heads. Then I turn Peyton around so I can look into her face. She cranes her neck, her eyes shining in the lights.

"Would you like me to take you up there?" I ask.

I'm teasing her. Never in a million years would I go up such a high tower and willingly strap myself into a ride like that.

Peyton's eyes grow so wide; it looks like they're bulging. Then she says the last thing I expected. "Let's go!"

Horror floods through me.

Before I can react, Peyton grabs my hand and runs across the street, dragging me with her. My stomach is a tangled mess and as we enter the elevator. All I can think about is that I'm going to need another drink.

# PEYTON

*I* wake up in bed aching in ways I never thought possible. My head, in particular, is thumping.

I squint against the harsh sunlight and rub my eyes. My fingers come away with dark smudge from the day-old mascara still clumping my lashes together.

I groan, sit up in bed, and stretch out with a yawn.

Then I blink through my clumpy lashes and spot something sparkly on my hand. That's when I see them.

A diamond ring, sitting next to a plain band, on my wedding finger.

A mixture of horror and excitement

bubbles up to the surface as I inspect the pretty rings. First of all, they look incredibly expensive. Second, I don't even remember putting them on.

Did Sebastian put them on me while I was asleep?

His name sparks a memory. A long, carpeted hallway lined with doors, and me in Sebastian's arms. Sebastian opening one of the doors and taking me in.

I giggled and made some cheesy remark about being Mrs. Rockwood and keeping up with traditions. Then the memory fades to nothing. I can't remember what happened next.

I rub my sore head and swing my legs out of bed, trying to make sense of the jumbled images floating in and out of my head.

When I look down at myself, I see bare thighs and a blue shirt.

*Oh no.*

Not just any shirt. Sebastian's shirt. I pull the collar up to my nose and sniff. His familiar scent floods me.

"No!" I breathe. There's a trail of clothes on the floor. My clothes. I start moving around quickly to retrieve them.

What did I do last night? How much did I have to drink? Why can't I remember?

Maybe I did something so embarrassing, my brain is repressing the memories for my own mental wellbeing.

When I'm done picking up after myself, I hurry into the shower and put it on the hottest setting that I can stand, hoping the scolding water will wash away any evidence of whatever happened last night.

Did we sleep together? That wasn't supposed to happen. The contract was *very* specific about that. But I've never been so drunk in my life. Who knows what drunk Peyton is capable of?

*It could be worse*, I tell myself.

I could have woken up with Sebastian in bed *with* me.

The fact that I woke up alone has to be a good sign. The thought offers me a little hope that maybe, just maybe, nothing happened at all and I'm jumping to conclusions.

*Oh no.*

I gulp.

*Did Sebastian see my Miss Piggy panties?*

I will die a thousand times over if he did.

I don't know why I chose those panties to wear on my wedding day, of all days!

Although, to be fair, I never dreamed that my boss would see me in them. Married or not.

The contract stated we wouldn't need to consummate the marriage, so it should have been perfectly safe to wear whatever character panties I liked.

I step out of the steamy bathroom, yank the towel around me and look around the room for my gym bag. It's nowhere to be seen.

I nip my bottom lip and wince. It's probably in the main room.

What if Sebastian is awake in there?

I figure walking out in his fancy button up would be more humiliating, so I tighten the towel around me to preserve whatever shred of my modesty is left, and open the door a crack to look inside.

Morning sunlight is flowing into the kitchen and TV area. I do a quick scout of the room. Nothing on the sleek leather couches or on the glass coffee table. I turn to the abandoned kitchen and breakfast bar. A flood of relief washes through me at the sight of my gym bag propped up by one of the bar stools.

There's no Sebastian in sight, so I creep over to my gym bag and grab the handles.

"Good morning."

*I* jump and lurch upward, banging my head on the granite of the overhanging breakfast bar. My thumping headache is a splitting one now, but the pain does nothing to dull the sheer horror of the sound of Sebastian's voice coming from behind me.

Quick as a flash, Sebastian's hands are on my forearms. I'm wrapped up in his woody scent and masculine pheromones, and his body is lightly pressed up against my butt. I straighten my spine, but he doesn't let me go. I feel his hard chest against my back and hold my breath while he inspects my head.

"Are you always this clumsy? That's the second time you've hurt yourself in twenty-four hours." The irritation in his voice makes me grit my teeth.

"I didn't hurt myself yesterday."

"Only because I caught you."

My breath hitches at the memory of

Sebastian's big hands on my waist, clutching me tight.

Today, there's nothing but a towel between his hands and my naked body. We're moving pretty quickly for a couple playing pretend.

I gulp.

He releases me and takes a step back like he just read my mind.

Slowly, I turn to meet his concerned gaze. He's not done telling me off.

"You need to be more careful. Do you not know how much you are worth to me?" His voice is soft now.

I open and close my mouth several times. At first, my brain tells me this is a declaration of love. But then I remember the contract. Our marriage. And the reason why he wants me to be his wife in the first place.

"Sorry," I blurt, fisting my towel and praying I don't do something clumsy again.

"I came out for my bag and…"

I stop talking when my brain registers the fact that Sebastian is shirtless.

He's standing in a pair of gray suit pants that are sitting just low enough on his waist for me to see a neat line of dark hair running up to his belly button. My cheeks burn as I take in all the details of his upper torso. My mouth goes dry and I speak quickly to try to defuse the energy I feel building in the room. "What are you doing without a shirt on?" I ask, sounding like a reproachful mom. Now it's my turn to be doing the telling off.

Sebastian's thick brows rise and the corner of his mouth lifts in a smirk. Then he holds up a shirt. "I came in here for the iron."

I blink several times. The guy presses his own clothes. I'm not going to lie, that's attractive.

I shake the silly thought out of my mind. "Couldn't you have worn your pajamas?"

Sebastian's smirk widens. "Actually, I sleep naked. I figured you would not appreciate bumping into me like that first thing in the morning."

Before I can stop myself, a strange noise escapes my mouth as a mental image of Sebastian without clothes presents itself to me.

The vision lasts for a split second before my rational brain kicks in. I clear my throat. "Right. You're right. This is better."

I can't look at him now. I glance from the

TV screen on the wall, to the portrait of a giraffe hanging by my bedroom door.

I don't need to look at him to sense his amusement. He chuckles.

I swear, if I wasn't standing in just a towel with a banging headache, I'd laugh too. The sound of his chuckle is the nicest thing to hear in the morning.

I force my gaze to meet his eyes one more time as I muster the courage to ask him my burning question.

"Did we…?" I motion to us both. "You know… Last night."

Sebastian's smile fades. He moves away to pull out an ironing board from a cupboard. "Did we what?" He asks with his back to me. He's suddenly very busy with his shirt.

I gasp.

"Please don't tell me we did anything last night. I don't remember."

Sebastian's head swivels on his neck. "You don't?"

I can't tell if he sounds relieved or disappointed, but the pitch in his voice is too high to sound normal.

I tuck my damp hair behind my ear and shuffle toward the door to my room, humiliation rising from my core. The way he's acting right now, coupled with the way I feel, is making me think we *did* do something.

I shut my eyes, praying I'm wrong. I can't be that woman who slept with her boss on a drunken night out and forgot about it in the morning. I mean, I'm already that woman who married her boss for money. There is no part of my sane mind that would want to make that any worse. But who knows what drunk Peyton thought was appropriate at the time? I haven't drunk like that since college. And I am definitely never drinking like that again.

"I woke up wearing your shirt and aching all over, so I thought…" I begin to explain, but I trail off at the sound of my voice. Saying it out loud makes everything a million times worse. I shut my mouth, unable to finish the thought.

Sebastian turns his attention to his shirt again and his cheeks grow crimson.

"Nothing happened last night." The bulge in his jaw is telling me something else.

Is he sparing my feelings? Does he think I'll go along with the lie?

"Do you remember what we did?" I ask.

Sebastian sets the iron down and pulls on his shirt. I watch him fasten the buttons over his defined abs.

I'm sure I'd remember touching them. It seems such a waste to think that I was that close and didn't collect any memories of it.

I grit my teeth. No. I am *not* attracted to my boss. I've never thought about him that way. Why do I keep getting these thoughts now?

Sebastian tucks in his shirt and drags a hand through his dark hair. "You wanted to go up the Strat."

"The what?" I squint at him, and part of me wonders if the "Strat" is some kind of British euphemism.

My eyes flicker to his crotch for the briefest second before I wrestle with my self-control and make eye contact again. Sebastian's smirk is back.

*Dang. He noticed.*

"The big tower with the rides on it?"

He points out the window and I take a look. "Oh," I say, the memory flooding back. "That's right."

I rub my temple and shut my eyes. "I do

remember sitting in a ride, and you holding my hand."

Sebastian chuckles again and my eyes open with a flash of concern. I can't help but get the feeling he's remembering something else. Did I puke? Did I freak out and make a scene? "What? What happened next?" I demand.

Sebastian walks over to the coffee maker in the kitchen and his expression turns serious. "I'm going to order breakfast. Go and get dressed."

I frown at him and want to argue that I'm not a child. Or somebody he can just boss around.

But I suddenly remember I'm standing in just a towel, and the water dripping from my hair is forming a small puddle by my feet. Besides all that, he's still my boss. Bossing me around is pretty much what he's been doing for the past decade.

I forgot that tiny detail somehow.

"Yes, Mr. Rockwood," I say on autopilot as I settle back into my role.

He gives me a hard look as I bend to pick up my gym bag. The intensity of his stare, now dark and brooding, hits me somewhere in the gut. "You must stop calling me that. I'm not Mr. Rockwood to you. Not anymore." His voice is low and commanding.

I hold his gaze for several moments. This whole thing is a lot more confusing than I thought it would be. I'm every shade of confused, but I nod. "Yes... Sebastian."

# SEBASTIAN

*P*eyton is nothing like the person I thought she was. At least, not when she's had a few drinks.

When she's drunk, she's loud and daring.

Last night, she grabbed my hand at every opportunity. I was grateful for that when we were on the top of the Strat.

Even with alcohol dulling my senses, I was very aware of how high up we were. The only thing that kept me calm up there was the warmth of Peyton's hand in mine.

She squealed and giggled as we walked up and down the strip more times than was necessary. She pointed at everything in awe and gave me a dedicated commentary of everything that went through her mind.

Which was a lot.

Her conversation ran like a train through endless topics that somehow connected together in her head. We went from theme park rides to cotton candy to candles, and then she mentioned a parrot named Larry and started doing impressions of all the characters in The Muppets.

Her Miss Piggy impression was the most impressive.

Peyton emerges fully dressed, with her dark hair in a messy bun at the top of her head. I try to keep my attention on tipping the hotel porter that's arrived with our breakfast.

After I close the door, I turn to see Peyton has already helped herself to a stack of blueberry pancakes.

"How did you know these are my favorite?" she asks between bites. Her cheeks are bulging like a hamster.

In truth, I didn't. I ordered everything on the breakfast menu in hopes that there would be something on it that she liked. But I make a mental note of blueberry pancakes, for next time. *Peyton loves blueberry pancakes.*

She apparently loves them so much, there may not be a single one left for me...

I suppress a smile and join her at the table.

"So, you really have no memories of last night?" I ask, helping myself to some bacon and eggs.

Peyton's eyes flash and she pauses mid-bite. Then she swallows and dabs her mouth with a table napkin. "I remember this." She holds up her left hand to show me the rings on her wedding finger. I nod slowly.

"Well, that is the most important memory."

Peyton's right brow arches. "It is?"

I incline my head. "For the immigration office. They'll be interested to know about our wedding." And so will my solicitor, I add silently.

Peyton pokes out her tongue and drags it across her bottom lip. Something funny happens to my insides. Why does that keep happening?

Then she picks up a glass of orange juice and I watch her take a thoughtful gulp. The sight brings back an image of last night. When I carried her into the suite, she licked her lips and gave me a hungry look.

Peyton slams the empty glass on the table with a bang and I snap out of my thoughts.

"I have to know, otherwise I'm going to lose my mind..." she says. Her cheeks turning red. I stare at her.

She wants to know if we slept together. I catch her eyeing up my body and it stirs something inside of me again, but I swallow hard and shift in my seat to suppress it.

"Nothing happened," I insist. But Peyton's right brow is not backing down. She's suspicious and I know she has every right to be.

"Something must have happened. I woke up wearing your shirt."

Her cheeks are flaming now and she's blinking faster than usual. I resist the urge to smirk. In all these years of working together, I've never seen Peyton so unraveled and frustrated. It's cute.

After a short staring contest, I come to the conclusion that she's not going to let the conversation drop until I tell her everything I know.

I puff out a deep breath. "Fine, but you won't like what you hear."

Peyton crosses her arms. "I just need to know the truth."

I scratch the back of my neck, sit upright, and avert my eyes. "You forced me onto all the rides at the top of the Strat." I try to keep my expression neutral while I recount that horror. Alcohol and motion are a terrible mix; it's amazing neither of us puked. "Then you wanted to watch a show and came onto one of the Blue Men afterward. I think your comment was that he looked like a 'buff smurf'."

Peyton's hand flies to her open mouth. "What?"

I chuckle. That's not even the worst of it.

"You got into a fight with a woman about animal cruelty, and you kept asking people where to find an 'adult pool' so you could swim... How did you put it? Ah yes, 'free from the confines of societal norms regarding nakedness.'"

Two hands are pressed over Peyton's mouth now, but they do not conceal her horrified groan. I raise a hand. "Don't worry, we didn't go to one. I took that as a sign to call it a night. So, I called a cab."

Peyton's eyes narrow on me. "But why was I..."

"Wearing my shirt?" I ask.

I avert my gaze, recounting the events of the tail end of last night.

Peyton was in my arms, and her hands were clasped behind my neck as I kicked the door open and walked in. She giggled, threw her head back and said, "I almost believe the lie. We got married today."

"We *did* get married today, that's the truth," I said, carrying her across to the bedroom.

Peyton took one look at the king-sized bed and gasped.

"That bed is bigger than my apartment!"

I set her down and she threw herself onto the mattress, her limbs stretched out in all directions. "What are you doing?" I asked.

She rolled onto her back and dragged her arms and legs up and down like wipers. "I'm making bed angels."

I snorted. Then I watched her act like a kid on a snow day for a few moments, wondering whether she was safe to leave in this state. When she stopped and sat up, her face turned serious.

"I'm your wife now for three hundred and sixty-five days, yes?"

I nod. "Correct."

Peyton pulled out her ponytail and a cascade of dark hair fell past her shoulders. Then she yanked her shirt over her head and tossed it to the floor like a rag. I stood there stunned. My shy, reserved personal assistant was looking me dead in the eyes and undressing.

She was unabashed by the moment. My eyes took in her exposed curves and paused when it registered that she was wearing a matching Miss Piggy panties and bra set. The Muppet's huge eyes were staring at me as Peyton moved closer on the bed, and it took all of my restraint not to laugh.

But then my eyes met Peyton's as she pulled herself up less than a foot away from me. She placed a hand on my shoulder and the heat from that touch spread all the way down my body.

"Well, let's get this over with," she said.

"What?" I asked, still frozen.

Peyton tutted and cocked her head to the side. She lowered her gaze to my chest. "The immigration interview… They'll want to know if we did it on our wedding night."

I swallowed. "I made it very clear in the contract that you're not expected to…"

Peyton's eyes flashed with anger as they found my gaze again and I lost my voice.

"Listen to me, Sebastian." Her voice turned silky when she uttered my name. "You are a terrible liar." She moved closer. Her heaving chest was now mere inches from mine, and every molecule in my body had started to buzz. "If you want to tell the immigration office that you had your wicked way with me on our wedding night..."

*Wicked way?* I thought. The corner of my mouth lifted in spite of the gravity of the moment. She noticed, and must have taken it as some sort of green light. Because the next thing I knew, she was unbuttoning my shirt. Suddenly, nothing was funny anymore.

"Peyton, stop." I grabbed her wrists and gave her a hard look. She stared back, her hooded eyes hungry and intense. Then she slid her tongue across her bottom lip and lowered her gaze to my mouth.

I stiffened, heat blazing all over me. Did she *really* want this?

But then my brain woke up and I shook myself. Allowing that thought to take root in my mind would have been a disaster.

Peyton unbuttoned the rest of my shirt

and slid it off my shoulders before I could react. I broke out into a nervous sweat. She brushed a hand across my chest and stretched to whisper in my ear. "Fine. You don't want to sleep with your wife. I'll honor your wishes. But at least let me borrow your shirt."

By the time I'm done recounting the night to a horrified Peyton, her hands are clamped firmly over her mouth. I don't think there is a single part of her face that isn't pink.

I lift my drink. "I did warn you."

I hadn't planned to tell her what happened. The fact that she had no memory at all this morning made me certain I did the right thing last night. There was no way I would have taken advantage of her drunken state. I may not have a lot of experience in the love department, but I know not to take advantage when a woman is vulnerable.

The memory of her curled up in my shirt as I tucked her into bed makes my heart thump faster. But I push it out of my mind to study a shell-shocked Peyton. "I can't believe I did those things. Said those things…" she says, finally lowering her hands.

I give an impassive shrug in the attempt to play it down. But Peyton's embarrassment is going to need more than a nonchalant reaction.

Time to change the topic. "Our flight leaves at six. What do you want to do today?"

Peyton's cheeks are still pink and she can no longer look me in the eye. "Well, I don't know. It sounds like we did everything last night," she says, looking at her plate.

"Not everything," I blurt before my brain can stop me.

Now it's my turn to feel heat rising to my face. Peyton looks at me with wide eyes.

# PEYTON

*I*f I didn't know any better, I'd have thought Sebastian was lying about last night. But he's a terrible liar.

Plus, the more I think about it, the more I remember.

I remember taking off Sebastian's shirt - the firm muscles under my fingertips as I dragged it down his arms. I remember his pectorals were clammy with sweat when I pressed up against him and whispered in his ear.

At the time, I thought I was being sexy and cool. Now, in the daylight, I'm mortified.

Sebastian is still my boss, and our

marriage is a sham. What on Earth made me come on to him like that?

I'm never drinking again. Ever. Not while I'm in this marriage.

Because there's no telling what I'll do next time.

Sebastian and I spent the rest of the day in the hotel suite. It took several hours of lying with a wet cloth over my eyes before my head would stop thumping. Sebastian set up an office by the window and pored over work.

I've wondered how long he can go without reading a manuscript or checking his emails. Not very long.

I'm still humiliated by the way I behaved.

How could I let myself get so out of control?

The truth is, it took several shots to find the courage to walk down the aisle. And every time the stark reality of my situation hit me, I'd grab another drink. That's how I ended up dazed and confused last night.

I've married my boss.

I'm officially Mrs. Rockwood.

Larry's squawky voice enters my head. "Crazy lady. Crazy lady."

And now that I can't turn to alcohol to

cope with the situation, the reality of my situation is like an alarm bell in my head. The fact is, I'm in this marriage for another three hundred and sixty-four days.

I'm going to eat healthy. Meditate. Take yoga breaths.

Anything except alcohol to help me cope.

The next hurdle isn't an easy one either; now that we're married, I have to move in with my new husband.

We're sitting in silence on the plane when Larry springs to mind again. "By the way, I have a pet," I say, turning to face Sebastian for the first time in several hours.

He hums deeply, but his eyes are still fixed on the screen in front of him. "I know. You told me everything last night. I've taken the liberty of making all of the arrangements to move you in."

I gawp at him. "What does that mean?"

He glances at me for the briefest moment, then his expression turns hard and he looks out the window. "Your neighbor had a spare key, so I've arranged for your parrot to be transported to my home and for your apartment to be cleaned out. Everything should be in order by the time we get back."

"Cleaned out? You mean…" A deep sense of dread rises in the form of pins and needles in my arms, and I start to panic at the thought of total strangers going through the darkest corners of my apartment.

"You'll find everything is at your new residence. And I've put the apartment up for rent. You're not going to be needing it for a year, after all."

My mind reels and my blood starts to boil. "What makes you think you can just take over my…" Sebastian looks at me and lifts his left hand. His gold ring flashes in the LED lights. I open and close my mouth silently.

"So, you think you can just take over my life now that I'm your wife?"

Sebastian's eyes flash and he looks around the cabin at the people surrounding us. I snap my mouth shut again. I forgot we weren't alone.

He leans forward, so close now that his lips brush my cheek as he murmurs into my ear.

"Don't forget your role, Mrs. Rockwood."

The warning tone in his voice sends a shiver down my spine and my heartbeat picks up. I gulp as he pulls back to look into my eyes again. "Let me get a few things straight," he says, keeping his voice low and quiet. Each word lands like a thunderclap on my ears. "Did you really think I was going to let you go back to that place? It's a death trap."

My insides squirm under his intense stare. But he's not done.

"You are my wife now. It is my job to take care of your needs."

I pull in a breath. "And is it my job to take care of yours?" I whisper back, meeting his hard stare. The side of his jaw bulges and his eyes flash.

Finally, after a long, heavy silence, Sebastian answers me with one word.

"Yes."

# SEBASTIAN

*I*t's been a day. One day, and already the tension between me and Peyton is so thick you could cut it with a knife.

How we're both going to get through a year is beyond my comprehension.

I had stipulated in the contract that this would be nothing more than a business transaction. There would be no shared bedroom, no physical contact away from the public eye, no relationship.

And absolutely no sex.

Yet, just a day into our marriage, I'm already starting to rethink all of my choices.

I have half a mind to tear up the contract and call the whole thing off. It's too risky. I was wrong about Peyton.

She's not just my meek, submissive PA, happy to pretend to be my wife for a life-changing paycheck.

She's got a feisty, independent side to her. A side that talks back.

And I have to admit, this side of her makes my heart race.

I don't know what gave her the courage to behave this way. At first, I thought it was the alcohol, but she's not had a single drop all day and still she looks at me with sass.

I expected she'd be grateful that I arranged for a team to pack up her apartment and move her in while we were away. Who would want to do all that themselves?

Instead, she's *irritated* with me. As if I've somehow been insensitive to her feelings, which is the total opposite to what I intended to do!

I'm not used to being challenged like this. Plus, I never expected to have such a reaction every time we touch. It's like an electrical charge that makes everything buzz.

There would be no sense in backing out now. The marriage papers are signed; her possessions are in my home. We've come this far, we'll just have to stick to the plan.

But if I'm to survive the next year without developing a stomach ulcer, I'll need to keep her close enough to protect her, but far enough to protect myself.

Easier said than done.

As far as she's concerned, we're acting like a couple for the immigration office. That means we need to behave like newlyweds when we're in the public eye.

And the more time I spend holding her hand, the harder it is to let go. It almost frightens me. If I don't figure out a way to cool things between us, it won't be long before I start to develop *feelings* and then I'll probably throw the rule book out the window.

I can't let that happen. With feelings in play, our arrangement is in jeopardy. She might start to think this marriage is real. Or worse, we might enter a real relationship and then when it inevitably falls apart—because we're not a good fit—it'll be the messiest divorce. And who's to say she'll stay the full year? After a bitter break up, she might not care about the money and just walk away. Then I'm back to square one, with a failed marriage on my record and scars on my heart. No. We can't get too close.

Luckily, I'm an expert at shutting off my emotions.

I've been avoiding my dad and stepmother for years, with relative success. Except for the obligatory holiday cards, and a quick phone call twice a year, I have nothing to do with them.

But it's easy to do that to people you can't stand being around. I've never been able to forgive my dad for moving on so fast.

If I lost my wife of twenty-three years, I would be a monk for the rest of my life. Like my grandpa.

But my dad didn't even wait for a headstone to be fitted before he married his secretary.

The stark realization that I've just married my PA hits me square between the eyes. I swallow against the lump in my throat and try to focus on the road ahead of me.

I've become my father.

I shake the thought away and grimace. I am *nothing* like him.

He takes nothing seriously. And in all these years, I've never once heard him even speak my mother's name. It was too distressing for Grandpa to talk about someone he'd loved so much and lost. My father pretends my mother didn't even exist. The difference is subtle, but it's there.

I clear my mind of bitter thoughts and pull up to the gate of my estate. The security guard waves and the iron gates open up to let me through. Peyton lets out a soft gasp. "This is your home?"

"It's *our* home," I correct her.

She repeats it under her breath as I park outside the front. "How many bedrooms do you have here?"

"More than we need."

I let her in through the double oak doors and we walk into the entrance hall. There's a sparkle in Peyton's eye as she takes all of it in. When she looks up at the chandelier, the lights dance off the marble floor and reflect on her face.

"This place is like something out of a movie," Peyton breathes.

I take her on a quick tour, keeping my voice professional. "This is the kitchen. I have a cook who is happy to prepare anything you need. Just ask. Your wing of the house is right next to the kitchen."

Peyton stays quiet and looks around with wide eyes as I show her the TV room, gym, and office on her side of the house. Then I open up her bedroom and she steps inside with a wistful look on her face that I don't fully understand. She looks like she's evaluating her cell.

A twinge of guilt nips at my insides, but then I recall the fact that I'm paying this woman one million dollars to stay in her own wing of the house. Not to mention all the extra expenses. It's hardly a prison.

"Where's Larry?" she asks, looking at the empty bird cage. I jerk my thumb over my shoulder.

"He's in the aviary with the other birds."

Peyton's eyes stretch wide. "You keep birds? How did I not know that?"

I shrug. "I guess there's still a lot you don't know about me, huh?"

Her brows are knitted together and her eyes are shifty.

"Do you want to see him?" I offer, trying to make eye contact.

Peyton jumps and looks at me. "Who?"

"Larry." I stuff my hands in my pockets and she breaks into a laugh.

"Oh, right. Yes. I want to see him."

# PEYTON

*I* thought I knew everything about my boss. Except for his first name, I suppose.

But I never guessed he'd be the type to keep birds.

I'm the only person in my social circle that has a pet like Larry.

What are the odds that Sebastian has a love for birds too?

He leads me into a landscaped yard.

Tall, evergreen trees stand like guards, and there are flowerbeds dotted about. A stone fountain sits pretty in the center, and there's a line of stepping stones in lush green grass, leading to a huge metal aviary. If I didn't know any better, I would have thought Sebastian had brought me to an estate in the British countryside. This certainly does not look like the outskirts of Manhattan.

We walk toward the aviary and the birdsong is so loud, I don't notice Larry's voice.

He's sitting in a prime spot, perched in the middle of a flock of yellow cardinals.

And he's singing Old McDonald.

Why is he singing Old McDonald?

He's standing with his wings folded neatly and his feathers down – a sign that he's happy and content.

Which is odd, because I always thought Larry hated other birds.

One time, back at my apartment, a pigeon perched on the open window and Larry screeched "get off!" until it flew away.

Then there was the time a nature program was showing on TV. When it started talking about birds of prey, Larry eyed the TV and shouted "Alexa, change the channel."

But here he is. His green and yellow feathers shimmer in the sunshine as he sways from side to side, serenading the cardinals.

"He's got a good pair of lungs on him,"

Sebastian points out. "And I have to say, his vocabulary is astounding."

I crack a smile. "You could say that. He doesn't shut up."

Sebastian unlocks the gate and I grab his arm before I can stop myself. "Aren't you worried about the birds flying away?" I blurt. His chocolate brown eyes lower to my hand on his arm and I let go. But then he drags his eyes upward to meet mine and his face settles into a contented smile. "They're in the cage by choice, not because I've locked them up."

"Are you insane?" I blurt. "Given half a chance, Larry would swoop out of there and fly off into the sunset. But not before squawking something sassy like "See you later, suckers!"

Sebastian chuckles.

There it is again. That dimple on his left cheek and the little crease between his brows that show whenever he lets out a laugh. I've worked with this man for a decade and the whole time, he's been grumpy and serious. Now, he's chuckling. And I'm not even trying to be funny.

He opens the gate and Larry stops singing, but he remains on his perch. He keeps a beady eye on Sebastian as the man enters the cage. I stare open-mouthed, waiting for a flood of yellow to shoot out into the air.

The strangest thing happens instead.

The yellow cardinals flock to Sebastian.

One of them sits on his head. Others perch on his broad shoulders. Within a few seconds, he's covered in birds.

Not only that, but he smiles at the birds like he's greeting old friends. Then he mumbles something inaudible to all of them. The depth of his voice is so low, it's dripping with masculine pheromones. And it's only then that I realize the yellow cardinals are all female.

How do I know?

Because Larry is still on his perch, but he's turned his back to Sebastian and is keeping dead silent.

Now it's my time to laugh. "I think you've offended my parrot; you've taken away all his lady friends."

Sebastian follows my line of sight and the corner of his mouth tilts up in a lopsided smirk. Then he looks at me.

"Now he knows who the alpha male is."

His words make my stomach squirm and I

don't know whether to be aroused or amused. But seeing as he's still got thirty birds perched all over his upper body, I go with the latter.

I mean, come on. Nobody can take a guy seriously when he looks like the crazy bird lady in Home Alone 2.

He notices my reaction before I can conceal it, and his expression hardens. He snaps his fingers and the birds take off to the top of the aviary. He brushes off his shoulders, then makes a beeline for me, his eyes dark and intense.

I stagger backward. He shuts the aviary door and moves even closer to me. I back-step until I hit a wall. Sebastian is so close to me now that the tips of his leather shoes are kissing my sneakers. I can feel his hot breath on my cheeks.

The birds have started to sing again, but nothing can drown out the sound of my heart thumping as Sebastian hovers over me, eyeing me up and down like I'm a snack. I can't move a single muscle.

"Want to tell me what's so funny?" he asks. His voice rumbles in my chest.

I want to tuck my hair behind my ear or find something else to do with my hands, but I resist the urge to move. He's so close to me, I might accidentally brush his cheek.

"Just the thought of you being an alpha to the birds… It's funny," I mumble awkwardly, trying and failing to avoid eye contact.

Sebastian places two palms on the wall on either side of my face. Then he leans in. "An alpha must assert his dominance on all living members of the home. Don't you agree?"

His eyes are holding me captive, and it takes all of my energy to nod. One second, we were both laughing, now I can't remember anything being funny.

The dimple is gone, but his bushy brows are knitted together, deepening the crease between them. My brain hasn't caught up with his sudden shift in mood, yet.

When he blinks, I'm released from his spell just long enough to grow dizzy.

Then he closes in on my ear and his stubble grazes my cheek.

"Don't forget who your alpha is, Peyton," he whispers in my ear.

I swallow and shake my head.

After a lingering pause, which turns out to be the most intense staring contest I've ever had, Sebastian drops his hands and steps back. My insides feel funny.

"As you can see, your parrot is fine. Now, don't stay out here too long. We've got work in the morning and a long week ahead of us."

I nod, wrangling my hands and trying to hide the fact that I'm shaking.

Sebastian rolls back his shoulders with a grunt. "I have a couple of manuscripts to read before bed. Do you think you can find your way back to your room?" he asks, but he's not looking at me now. His gaze is hovering an inch above the top of my head.

"Yes," is all I can say. And even that tiny word comes out in a squeak. I muster courage and try again. "I'll be fine."

# SEBASTIAN

*A*fter reading the same sentence fifty times, I close my laptop and bury my head in my hands. Even work can't distract me.

Reading usually silences my thoughts, but nothing has worked so far to quiet the single thought running through my head.

Peyton Bishop is in my home.

Correction. *Mrs. Peyton Rockwood* is in my home.

The editor part of my brain wants to cross that out too and replace the last two words with *our home.*

I shake my head in a feeble attempt to

discard that thought, but it's like a barnacle on a ship.

*Our* home. Peyton is my wife.

I have to admit it. I'm confused. I thought I could push her away. Keep cool and aloof even. But within moments, she has me laughing.

Laughing! I can't remember the last person that made me laugh. Possibly my grandfather.

But then she laughed *at* me in the aviary and it reminded me of my father. The years he would talk down to me and make me the butt of his jokes in front of his friends. My father's cavalier attitude to life but eternal disapproval of me is probably what gave me my deep-rooted need for respect.

In New York, I'm respected. No one laughs at me here. The moment I saw that look on her face, the need to put Peyton in her place became all-consuming.

But by the time I was done, there was fear in her eyes instead. That set off another chain reaction in my body - one that made me feel sick with guilt.

On the bright side, the experience offered me an idea.

Maybe if I act like a jerk, Peyton won't forget this is just business.

I was not in my right mind when I decided to marry her.

I thought I had no attraction toward her, that the arrangement would be simple. Apart from the actual wedding, I didn't think we'd have to do anything more than stay married for a year. I imagined we could live like distant roommates and continue working day-to-day, like we always have.

But I've presented myself with a magnificent problem. The problem is that I told her I chose her because she's American. She thinks we need to convince the immigration lawyers that we're a legitimate couple. So, now we'll have to pretend to be a couple in the public eye.

That would have been simple enough if we could play the part and keep our emotions out of it.

I didn't consider the possibility of a different Peyton; the one that let her hair down in Vegas and showed me her Miss Piggy underwear.

Now I can't *stop* thinking about her.

I groan into my arms.

I shouldn't have rushed into this.

It's not like I'm desperate for money. I could have left it all in trust until I found Mrs. Right and got married for real.

I sip my coffee and grimace at the cold, bitter taste. How many hours have I been here, poring over manuscripts?

Too many.

Especially considering the fact I've got an abysmal amount of work done and it's almost dawn.

When Grandma died, a man at the wake said, "Don't make any big decisions while you're grieving."

I thought it was odd advice at the time, but I see the wisdom of it now.

It's like the time, back in school, when my friend's uncle passed so he got a puppy. They weren't dog people in his family, and no one had the patience for when the labradoodle started to chew up all of their shoes and pee everywhere.

They soon saw sense and had it rehomed.

Then, there's my dad. He married his secretary before the dirt had even settled on my mother's grave.

People should have mental capacity tests done before a wedding.

How could I be allowed to make such a massive mistake?

But I guess that's why we went to Vegas in the first place. No one over there is bothered about whether their clients are of sound mind at the time of their nuptials. After all, most of the people who go to the Chapel of Bells are absolutely not in their right mind.

Case in point: Peyton got so drunk, she'd forgotten almost everything the next day.

And yet, here I am. Married to my PA. The thought sends a shiver down my spine.

In spite of every effort to distance myself from him, I have become my father's son.

My phone vibrates and drags me out of my self-destructive thoughts. I look at the caller ID and frown.

The solicitor. What does he want? The will has been read, and all of Grandpa's affairs were in hand.

"Mr. Rockwood, I wanted to talk to you about the particulars of your grandfather's estate."

I arch my back and stifle a yawn with my

fist. "It's all right, I have some news that should make all of this much simpler."

"Oh?"

I do my best to sound less formal as I break the news of my marriage, but it's clear that I'm fooling no one. My solicitor's voice drips with disapproval.

"You got married in Vegas."

It's not a question. It's a frank statement laced with disappointment.

"Listen, it's not your job to judge my actions." I stand up and square my shoulders as I start to pace my room. The soft pile carpet under my bare feet is a small comfort in this tense situation. If there's anything I hate more than making foolish choices, it's being judged for said foolish choices.

"There's nothing in the will to suggest that the marriage needed to be for love."

A low hum tells me I'm not wrong, but he's not going to admit it. "Listen, the spirit of the request was so that your grandfather…"

"I don't want to know why," I cut in.

"But if you have read the letter…"

"I haven't," I say through gritted teeth. I have no interest in the games my grandfather got up to in his twilight. "The point is, on

March twenty-first, next year, the assets will be released to me."

"And your wife," my solicitor adds. But I brush the thought aside. Peyton signed a pre-nup. She has no claim on that money even if there's a clause in the will that says my wife and I will have joint ownership.

"So, who is the lucky lady?"

I bite the inside of my cheek. "An old friend," I say.

It's not entirely false. Peyton has been working for me for many years; that's got to put us in as old acquaintances at the very least. The fact that she didn't know my first name until this week is beside the point. In truth, I've always kept people at a safe distance.

I like to keep conversations brief and professional. And I avoid small talk at all costs. Peyton was no exception.

Going by last names helps me focus on the work, not the workers.

In fact, now that I think about it, I'm not surprised that I don't know more about Peyton.

I have no idea how she likes her coffee, or

what her tells are when she's stressed. I never paid much attention.

But she was always there - waiting in the wings while I took meetings, quick to bring me a strong coffee when I was running low. She even knows when to reschedule my appointments because I'm having a terrible morning.

She's always been instinctive about her work. She stays late dutifully, keeps her desk immaculate and organized, and I've never seen her gossiping at the water dispenser.

I remember now why I chose her. She represents everything that I need for this arrangement. Commitment, respect, and obedience.

Of course, ever since we entered first name territory, things have changed.

She suddenly has opinions on everything - opinions that she's not afraid to share with me.

I still have the image of her Miss Piggy underwear burned into my cranium. It's an image that makes it increasingly difficult to look at her professionally.

I scratch the back of my neck as the droning tones of my solicitor's voice returns to my attention.

"If the marriage ends even a day before the first anniversary, the estate will not be handed over. So, Mr. Rockwood, if your marriage is disingenuous, I suggest that you work hard to..."

"I've got it."

He doesn't need to tell me. This marriage has high stakes. If Peyton and I end it early, it's game over.

Which just cements my decision to be a jerk, so she and I don't venture into new territory. I need to shut her out and stop flirting with her. She needs to keep seeing me as her boss. Never as her husband.

Although, I'm starting to see how striking the balance between being a jerk and an insufferable buffoon is going to be tricky.

Still, I'm sure I can manage. Especially with the next big event on my calendar looming.

In four hours, I'll take Peyton into the office and make a big announcement.

One that I'm not entirely excited to announce.

# PEYTON

Sebastian asserting his dominance over me left an impression. It took several hours for my heartbeat to return to normal, and I couldn't stop replaying the moment in my head.

How he can flip so suddenly from playful to authoritative is beyond me.

But it's hard to stay angry when I'm in the most comfortable bed ever. The baby-butt-soft sheets must be Egyptian cotton or something. And the mattress is hard enough to give my back support, but squishy enough to let my body sink.

I wriggle under the sheets with my eyes shut and sigh.

So, this is what luxury is like.

I can mimic a starfish and stretch out as far as I can, and my toes won't even reach the sides of the bed. There's something about being dragged out of my poor gal world and into this new luxurious life that makes me feel young again. I roll over and sniff the plush pillow. It floods my senses with a smell I can't name.

It's a fresh, floral laundry detergent mixed with something heavier that I can't name, like pinecones and rain.

My room is huge. And it's mine for the next eleven months and twenty-eight days. The massive floor to ceiling windows let in so much light, I woke with a start this morning, blinded by sunshine. Whoever thought sheer white curtains are practical is living on another planet.

But complaining about the lack of black-out drapes seems insensitive when there are people literally starving in the world.

The shrill ring of my alarm breaks the gentle tones of chirping from outside. My thoughts scatter. It's time to get ready for work.

I jab my phone with my thumb until the

jarring sound stops, then I shuffle off the giant bed and walk barefoot across the room. The carpet pile is so high; my strides leave footprints behind me.

The way my toes snuggle into the carpet brings a goofy smile to my face. Honestly, it's the little things in life.

At the end of this, I'll build my own house and have fancy carpets too.

My bathroom consists of a large, open shower; his and her sinks; marble tile walls and flooring; and glitzy mirrors surrounded by bulbs - like the ones you'd expect to see backstage on Broadway. Light dances off the polished tiles and glass.

This is the life.

I can see Sebastian and I co-existing in this massive house for a year. I'll be a millionaire at the end of it too. I smirk at the thought.

Maybe this arrangement isn't going to be so hard, after all.

*Who's the crazy lady now, Larry?*

The shower has so many handles, it takes me a hot minute to figure out how to turn it on. There's settings for a spray that makes me feel like I've stepped into a car wash. Some are jets that let out water in pulses. Then there's the huge showerhead above me that simulates rain.

Sebastian kept to his room for the rest of the evening yesterday, leaving me to watch TV in bed and try to distract myself from reality.

The living arrangements are great, but there is one tiny problem.

The immigration interview. Or *interviews*.

I've still got no idea how I can convincingly lie to them.

It's breaking the law. I'd be a felon if we're caught.

My brain concocts visions of me running through the damp streets of New York in all black, being chased from back alley to back alley by a mob of angry policemen.

Is all of this luxury worth the risk?

I'm of two minds as I take a shower and get ready for work. Just as I slip my shoes on, my stomach grumbles. I'm not usually the type of gal to eat breakfast, but ever since I became Mrs. Rockwood, my appetite has skyrocketed.

I don't know if it's comfort eating, or the fact that there's food in abundance. But I just can't stop.

All of the kitchen cupboards are full of

cans and snacks. There's even a huge supply
of candy bars; those won't last long while I'm
around.

I've never seen so much food.

And Sebastian's cook has filled the fridge
with meals ready to reheat in the microwave.
If I'm not careful, I'll be a million pounds
heavier by the end of this year.

I venture into the kitchen for a mug of
coffee and stop by the door at the sight of
Sebastian, in a dark suit, cradling a steaming
mug and looking out the tall pane windows.

"Sleep well?" he asks without shifting his gaze
from the window. I can't bring myself to
answer with words, so I settle for "Mm-hmm."

There's something about the way he's
standing, so cool and aloof, that reminds me
of the many mornings I've walked into his
office. And just like that, I'm back into my
role as his PA. He wouldn't so much as look
in my direction while I listed off all the
appointments for the day. I notice he's
wearing his red tie. It's the one he wears
when he wants to come across as confident
and assertive. The one he wears when he's
stressed.

His eyes find mine after he takes a sip

and then they size me up and down, like a pair of lasers carving up my body. I tug on my skirt.

"You're wearing that?" he asks.

I frown at the disdain in his voice.

"What's wrong with this?" I ask, smoothing my purple satin blouse. "This is what I always wear to work."

Sebastian sets his mug down and crosses his arms across his broad chest. "That was before you became my wife. Now you need to look the part."

I cock a brow. His power over me is fading. Irritation takes over. "Are you serious? Who cares what I look like?" Then a thought hits me like a smack to the face. "Do you think they'll interview people from work?"

Sebastian drops his arms. "Who?"

"You know, the immigration office," I reply, fiddling with the hem of my shirt. My stomach begins to churn again. There's so much I hadn't thought about.

Is this going to be a year of public appearances and grueling interrogations? I'm not sure I can handle the constant lies.

I was foolish to think that living in a house of luxury would make this a piece of cake.

My jaw tenses as I think about why I'm doing this. *One million dollars. Freedom.*

"Oh. Right." Sebastian rakes a hand through his hair. He must be following my train of thought because his shoulders sag. But he recovers in record speed and puts on his official expression. The kind he saves for his least favorite clients. "Exactly. I can't have you showing up to the office looking like my PA."

"But I *am* your PA," I correct him, my insides prickling.

Why does he have to be such a jerk? I mentally shake myself and put on my professional act. "Which reminds me, you've got an appointment with Cartwell at eight o'clock. We should get going..."

Sebastian hums with his brows knitted together. The way he does it is almost primal. "Cancel all my appointments for the morning," he orders, his eyes snaking all over my body. I cross my arms, unsettled by his gaze. It's like he can see through my clothes or something. I'm never wearing Miss Piggy panties ever again.

"Why?" I can barely get the word out of my lips. Sebastian meets my gaze and his expression is one hundred percent serious. "I'm taking you shopping."

I stare at him unblinking for a moment. "You-you don't need to do that," I stammer. He strides across the kitchen and towers over me, flooding my senses with his strong cologne. "Yes, I do," he growls. He places his hand on the door behind me and leans in. "It's important we make it intrinsically clear to everyone at the office, the staff, the cleaners, and even the janitor... That you belong to me."

I gulp.

# SEBASTIAN

*L*etting Peyton loose with my credit card bought me time to fix a growing problem.

What she thinks is we're trying to prove ourselves to the Immigration office. And to stop her asking too many questions, or letting the real reason for the marriage slip, I need to keep up with the lie.

Now I'll have to research what the immigration process entails when it involves getting married to an American citizen.

The truth is, I have three businesses in my name with thousands of employees. That was enough to earn residency. My immigration lawyer handled the process years ago.

Getting a marriage visa is an entirely different kettle of fish, though. The more research I do, the more I regret telling Peyton it was why I needed her.

But she can't know the truth. Not yet. I don't trust that she won't try something foolish. Pre-nup or no pre-nup, if she gets the idea in her head that she could stake a claim on billions of dollars, then there's no telling what she'll do. And I'm not just going to roll over and give away a chunk of Grandpa's estate to my PA.

She could hang this over my head all year if she knew. Torture me. Or worse, murder me in my sleep while we're still married and inherit it all.

My thoughts are a little grim today. But that's because I was up all night reading a psychological thriller about a narcissistic wife killing her husband and trying to get away with it.

In reality, Peyton isn't capable of murder. At least, I don't think so.

During the car ride to work, she asked a million questions about it. "I think we should make a folder and put together all of our likes and dislikes... Other stuff like our family history, maybe even make up some memories…" She rattled off a list of suggestions while I zoned out and began to sweat.

I hate lying.

It's not the best foundation for a relationship, and a year is a long time to lie to someone you live with. But I have no other choice. I've made this bed, now I have to lie in it.

While Peyton disappeared into the changing rooms with piles of clothes in her arms, I made a few calls.

Setting up actual meetings at the immigration office is out of the question, so I'll need to be more creative.

Luckily, I'm not short on contacts. I felt confident someone would know an actor who could be discreet and help me out.

Sure enough, one of my friends from the country club was able to help. His accountant enjoys improv on Tuesday evenings, and he just so happens to work in an office block that could pass for a lawyer's office.

I set up an appointment for next week. Then I drafted an email on my phone for him to print out and mail to me.

It's remarkable how many details there are

to consider when you're concocting a lie.

By the time Peyton returns, I've already sent the email with a list of instructions, put down a substantial deposit and called my friend back to thank him for the contact.

"Are you happy?" I ask. Peyton peeks out from behind a bundle of clothes and frowns.

"I don't know if I like the wide leg pants or the pencil skirt better."

I shrug. "Whatever you don't wear today, you can wear tomorrow."

Peyton looks alarmed. She doesn't have to say it. I can see by the look on her face that she was trying to choose only one outfit to buy. I carefully take the pile of clothes from her. "You like all of these? They fit okay?" I ask.

Peyton's eyes go from my face to the clothes, and then up at me again. "That silk blouse costs more than I make in a week."

The statement makes my insides twist with guilt.

I can't help but notice the skinny shop assistant raising her tattooed brows in my direction. My discomfort grows. I turn back to Peyton and force a smile.

"Darling, you are my wife. I will buy you everything in this store if it makes you happy."

Peyton's brows travel up her forehead in surprise, then they come back down again as she frowns at me. I glance at the assistant, who is smiling now. Then I look back at Peyton. Peyton follows my line of sight. Her mouth makes a perfect o when she catches on.

"Well, if you're sure... I think I need to get this jacket in tan and chocolate brown too... darling."

She winks with a cheeky grin and I resist the urge to roll my eyes. Three jackets, four skirts, two dresses, five blouses, a faux fur coat, six pairs of shoes and two pairs of pantyhose later... We leave the designer store laden with bags.

"What about underwear?" I ask her as we walk the streets. Peyton's cheeks flush and she looks away. "What about it?"

"Well, do you need any?" I say, unable to stop the image of her matching Miss Piggy set from flooding my mind.

Peyton halts on the sidewalk, and the people milling around us start to grumble about her stopping the flow of traffic. "Listen,

I'm grateful for this," she lifts up the bags. "But I draw the line on underwear. You don't need to buy everything for me. I can get my own."

I lift a skeptical brow. She gives me a hard look, daring me to argue. I decide against it. It seems slightly inappropriate to squabble about underwear in the middle of New York City.

"Fine. Let's take these home and get ready for the office. I'm going to announce our marriage to the staff today."

Peyton's cheeks go a deeper shade of red. Then she grabs my arm as she starts to walk. "We should get a bite to eat first."

"It's only eleven," I say. In all the years I've worked with Peyton, she's never eaten before noon. And even then, all she does is eat a granola bar to get her through the rest of the workday.

Then I remember how she devoured that stack of blueberry pancakes back in Vegas. Maybe the stress is giving her an appetite.

A gust of wind blows her hair forward and she shakes it back. The air is so humid, it's almost wet. Another shower of rain must be on its way.

"If you want me to be in a good mood
and act like your doting new wife at the office,
I need cake," Peyton says, grinning now. "And
I know just the place."

# PEYTON

*E*lle's Kitchen is packed with people. But I manage to grab a table just as a couple is leaving. They'd barely got out of their seats before I was at their side, waiting and grinning like some weirdo.

I'm not gonna lie. Going on a shopping spree with someone else's credit card has given me a buzz. Now I want a triple chocolate cookie from Elle's Kitchen.

My mood is already looking up.

Sebastian takes a seat and carefully props my bags up against his legs under the table. "Have you been here before?" he asks, looking warily around at all the people squeezed into the small store.

I shake my head. "I walk past this place every day on the way back from work and I always think about coming in for a treat, but I never have."

Sebastian strokes his jaw absentmindedly, as though to ponder some deep meaning behind what I've said. The truth is, I never came in because I never had the spare change.

"On a fad diet?" he asks. I resist the urge to roll my eyes. Diets are for rich people. The idea of restricting yourself from delicious food on the basis of avoiding calories is a luxury I do not enjoy.

I skip meals so that I can pay the rent.

But Sebastian doesn't need to know that. And I won't need to worry about that anymore. The change is going to take some getting used to.

"Something like that," I shrug, trying to sound impassive. Sebastian gives me a discerning look.

"Hey, I haven't seen you two here before, welcome to Elle's Kitchen. I'm…"

I look up at the musical voice and my mouth drops open. "You're Elle Masters!" I squeak.

*Don't fangirl, Peyton.*

I shut my mouth and force a smile, trying to play it cool. But Elle looks at me with shining eyes. Her cheeks, for some reason, are turning pink. "Yes," she says in a breathy voice.

I notice the giant rock on her finger. The thing nearly blinds me when she moves her hand down to cradle a bump.

"Congratulations. Do you know what you're having?" I ask.

Elle follows my gaze and looks down at her bump, then laughs. "No. Zane and I wanted to keep it a surprise. But we've only been able to agree on a name for a girl, so I'm taking that as a sign."

My smile stiffens and Elle's voice fades as my mind pulls me into my past. Did my mom cradle me like that while I was still in the womb? Did she talk to strangers about how excited she was to paint the nursery? Or about the little squabbles she had with her husband over names?

The answer is no. I know that for certain. Because I grew up in foster care with almost no knowledge of who my birth parents were. The only thing I was told was their names.

I can't imagine that she told anyone about

the pregnancy. I wonder how she chose my name. Maybe she was a teenager watching One Tree Hill.

I was lucky to be raised by a loving couple, but they were in their sixties while I was in high school. Too old to really understand anything about my life so far past their own youth. They had both passed away before I graduated from college.

The trip down memory lane is a stark reminder of how alone I am.

Except for Larry. He's the only living reminder of the fact that my foster parents used to be in my life.

When I finally looked up my birth parents, I was too late. My dad had died from an overdose twenty years ago, and my mom had passed away in a car accident just a month before I found her.

My chest tightens and my eyes prickle with hot tears as I think about the past. I bite back against the painful memories and force my attention back to Elle, who is now speaking to Sebastian.

"So that's two milkshakes, and the nibble platter coming up."

She disappears through the crowd as she

makes her way to the counter. Sebastian's look of concern fills my vision. "Are you feeling okay?" he asks.

I shake myself. "I'm fine."

It's a lie. I'm not fine. The past still has my heart in a vise and I've suddenly lost my appetite.

"You don't look fine. You've gone pale," Sebastian insists. "You're worrying me."

I stare at my hands on the table. I can't remember the last time anyone worried about me. I've just been surviving, looking after myself and trying to bury my bad memories in a hole.

It's funny. Just when I think I've put it all behind me, something insignificant like Elle clutching her bump takes me right back and opens up all these old wounds.

Maybe I've got PTSD. If I had money for therapy, I'd know.

Anyway, I can't sit and wallow in self-pity over things that happened a million years ago. Nothing will change the past. Plus, Sebastian's deal is going to change everything.

Next year, I'll be able to start afresh. Free from debts and failures hanging around my neck. I won't be afraid of abandonment anymore, because Larry and I will live in a beautiful house in the country where no one can hurt us again.

But if I want to earn a million buckeroos, I'm gonna have to get a grip on my emotions and put on a smile.

My heart won't stop racing and the familiar pins and needles on my arms are telling me a panic attack isn't far away.

Sebastian clears his throat and I blink up at him. He's giving me a strange look that I can't read. I wonder if he can read me.

"Why don't I tell you some things about me that you don't know?" he asks. His voice is soft now.

I interlock my fingers and squeeze my hands together. "Okay, fill me in on some personal details."

Sebastian's face turns amused. "*Personal* details?" he repeats. "Like what?"

Happy that we're talking about something I can focus on; I relax my shoulders. The panic is already fading. "Oh, I don't know. How about shoe size, for starters?"

Sebastian's mouth lifts into a smirk. "And *why* are you curious about my shoe size?"

We share a look for a long moment until I

can't stop a grin from taking my face. "It just seems like a detail your wife should know; don't you think? How else am I supposed to buy you slippers for your birthday?"

Sebastian laughs. I swear we're having two conversations. One with our words, another with our eyes.

A rush of giddiness floods me. It's a welcome change from the way I felt just moments earlier. I'm relieved to see he's showing his playful side again.

He leans forward, rests his elbows on the table and lowers his voice to a whisper. "Well, I do have rather large feet. Is that what you wanted to know?"

My heart thrums against my ribcage. Neither of us needs to say it, but I'm pretty sure neither of us are talking about feet anymore.

"That's… Good to know." I say in a voice as breathy as Elle's was earlier. Sebastian rakes me with his eyes again. It's like his eyes are heat lamps, warming anything in their path.

"You don't believe me? You want to see for yourself?"

My cheeks are flaming now. "No. I don't want to see your feet," I say quickly.

Sebastian holds my gaze, his eyes twinkling. I can tell by the tension in his jaw that he's holding back laughter.

And so am I. To anyone else, we'd sound like a couple of weirdos talking about feet. I can't stop grinning. He's distracting me on purpose, and it's working.

"What do you want to know about me?" I ask. Sebastian's smile turns almost devilish. "Everything."

# SEBASTIAN

*I* did my best to play the standoffish boss, but Peyton keeps unraveling me and bringing out my soft side.

The way she went white as a ghost when Elle touched her baby bump had me curious. What made her react that way? Something must have happened in her life to make a conversation with a pregnant woman so awkward.

She looked more vulnerable than I've ever seen her, biting her lip and hugging herself. Her breaths started to come quicker and I was worried she was about to faint.

Peyton is no use to me unconscious. So I got her laughing and talking about my feet.

Her giggle broke the hold of whatever it was she'd been battling in her head, and she started to talk at length. I stored all of the random facts she spilled in a memory bank in my mind.

She reads psychological thrillers and listens to true crime documentaries to calm down at night. That made me think; murdering me in my sleep is more of a possibility than I'd imagined.

Her favorite ice-cream is mint chocolate chip, and she'd never left New York until we went to Vegas.

Listening to Peyton was calming. By the time we got to the office, my stress levels had dropped significantly. But my heart started to hammer again when we got inside.

The office is usually my favorite place to be. People respect me here, and there's a strict rhythm in the way my day runs.

I sip my morning coffee while I look through emails, and Peyton goes through my agenda for the day. Then I meet with a couple of clients before a quick lunch, which is usually spent in a coffee shop with a literary agent.

The afternoon is when I catch up with

junior editors and agree to new projects. And when everyone is gone, I stay late and read manuscripts in peace.

The routine is out the window today though, and there's an uncomfortable tightness in my chest as I walk in with Peyton by my side.

My grandpa always said if you need to do something but you don't want to do it, treat it like a Band-Aid and rip it off fast.

So, the first thing I do is call a staff meeting.

"Thank you for coming," I say. I have the jitters, but I've managed to keep my voice steady so far. I can't decide if it's my nerves causing the jitters or a sugar rush from all the junk Peyton and I ate at the cake shop. I look out at the sea of faces in the conference hall. I wanted to announce our engagement via email; it's truly not that important for the staff to know. But Peyton thought it would be better to do it in person, so as to look more convincing. "For the immigration office." It's a phrase that's getting old, fast.

I snake my arm around Peyton's back and clutch her waist. Her hip bumps into mine. She's wearing one of her new outfits; a black pencil skirt and a silk, ivory blouse. I run my thumb across the silky material. She looks good in designer clothes, and her shapely figure sits nicely on me.

She flashes me a shy smile and tucks hair behind her ear. I turn back to the staff.

"I want to make a formal announcement so you hear this from me, and not the rumor mill," I explain.

Whispers sweep through the room like a Mexican wave. Peyton's hand is resting between my shoulder blades. Her fingernails dig into me like cat claws. I tense my jaw, trying not to think about the irrational pleasure her digging is triggering.

I wish I took the time to prepare myself for this announcement. But my mind is blank and all I can think about is how odd I must look to the staff. Here I am, clutching my PA. It's highly inappropriate. But Peyton's research was thorough. She insists that the immigration office will ask the staff about us. How can I let her know we don't need to worry about keeping up the façade, without telling her the truth?

No. We have to go along with Peyton's

plan. I hate it, but I'll just have to get it over with.

"Miss Bishop and I have been seeing each other for some time now, and this weekend we decided to tie the knot." I say it all so fast, I don't think I even stopped to take a breath.

There's an audible gasp from half of the staff. The other half are silent and staring at me and Peyton, dumbfounded.

She bursts out in a nervous giggle.

A hesitant clap follows and there's light chatter, but the awkwardness is rising. Now the news is out, I feel a rush of foolishness. I can see on the faces of my staff that they're thinking, '*You called a staff meeting for this?*'

Peyton and I exchange looks. We're not convincing anyone, and if we thought simply making an announcement would stop people from gossiping about us, we were wrong. My thoughts are validated when I catch the whisper of a couple of women to my side. "What do you think is really going on?"

"Any questions?" I ask.

A young woman shoots her hand in the air. "Will there be a party, sir?"

"Of course," Peyton announces before I can. I shoot her a look, but she's smiling at the crowd now. Her nails dig into my back with more pressure. "We'll have a party at the house, and everyone's invited."

Now the chatter rises in pitch. Instead of low mumbles, there's excited talk.

"I need to go shopping, I don't have a thing to wear!"

"Do we need to get them a gift?"

Too stunned to say anything more, I dismiss the meeting and watch people shuffle out of the room.

When we're alone again, I release my grip on Peyton's waist and raise a brow at her. "A party? Really?"

She shrugs and flicks her hair back. "You saw the way everyone was looking at us. We're not fooling anyone. But if we throw a party..." She clutches my arm with a squeal. "All those witness statements! Think about it. Everyone will be talking about it."

I pull in a breath to bury my disapproval. I don't much like these developments, but she's a woman who can think quickly on her feet. Announcing a party would be a good reason to gather all the staff for a meeting too.

She gives my arm another squeeze before she has mercy and lets it go. "Don't you

worry," she says, sounding like the Peyton
Bishop I've known all these years. "I'll take
care of the arrangements."

"You think you can handle it?" I ask. She
scoffs as we leave the room, then gives me one
of her discerning stares. "I've single-handedly
arranged book launches, Christmas parties,
and charity functions. This is what I do."

"Fine," I say, admitting defeat. "I'll leave it
to you. Just don't tire yourself out too much. I
still need you to do your actual job."

Peyton snorts as the elevator doors roll
back. A small group of junior editors are
standing inside it. They stare at us like deer
stuck in headlights. Peyton's smile widens and
she presses her cheek against mine while she
whispers into my ear.

"You underestimate what I can do, Mr.
Rockwood."

Her silky voice fills me with warmth. I
tense my jaw, trying to ignore the explosive
influence she's having on my body. Then she
moves away and links her arm with mine as
we enter the elevator.

"Did you see that?" one of the editors
whispers to the woman next to her. I stare

ahead blankly as the doors roll shut, but I strain my ears to catch the reply.

"I didn't just see it, I *felt* it. Wow."

I resist the urge to smile. My brain is working overtime. The closer I get to Peyton, the more walls I feel coming down... I need to play this very carefully. There's too much at stake.

I grind my teeth as I think about what I'm going to have to do. I'm pretty sure she's going to hate me for it, but I have no other choice.

Jeopardizing the plan is too costly.

# PEYTON

Over the next week, whispers followed me everywhere I walked. But in the same way, talking would stop as soon as I entered a room. On multiple occasions, the group of women huddled by the coffee machine scattered as I approached.

I've never made any friends at the workplace; being Sebastian's PA is a very intense job. I barely find time to pee, let alone gossip by the water dispenser.

Now I can't help but feel even more isolated. At least, before I became Mrs. Rockwood, I would get a passing smile or even an obligatory "How are you?"

Now, I get whispers and filthy looks like I'm a bad smell. Sebastian and I settled back into old habits at work, but with the added task of acting like a married couple around the staff. We've played our roles perfectly so far; it doesn't require a lot of physical contact because we keep things professional at the workplace anyway. Sebastian occasionally calls me darling. It's unusual enough to make me pause every time. Then I recover and shoot him a coy smile.

I don't think it'll ever feel normal to be called darling. Not by him.

But as soon as all the staff have gone home and we're the only ones in the office, Sebastian goes cold as ice.

I used the quiet time to focus on planning our party.

Friday night finally rolled around, and I can't help feeling more relieved than usual to see the weekend.

The stars are out tonight. When we arrive at the house, Sebastian looks at me for the first time in hours. "Did you get my email about the interview on Monday?" There's an edge to the tone of his voice.

I try to ignore the sickly feeling the reminder brings. "With immigration? Yes."

My stomach knots itself. We're not ready for the big interview. I'm sure of it. But the email stated it was just an introduction. My eyes linger on Sebastian as we head for the front door. His shoulders are tense; too high to look natural. And a vein on his temple is pulsing. He must be worried too.

"Don't worry," I say, putting on a brave smile. "We've got the weekend to get to know each other."

Sebastian's expression is unreadable when he looks at me. "I'm working all weekend."

Startled, I blink several times as I take in his response. "Wait," I say. "Aren't you concerned that we aren't prepared for this interview?"

Sebastian sighs as he opens the door and throws his bag on the counter. "Peyton, it's been a long week. I've still got a pile of paperwork to get through. The last thing I want to think about right now is a silly…"

"You think immigration is a joke?" I ask, balling my hands into fists. "I'm putting my neck on the line for you, and you're not even prepared to find out anything about me? I mean, you've barely talked to me all week!"

Sebastian swivels on the spot to give me a hard look. "Is that what you're worried about?" he asks. "That I haven't paid you enough *attention*? I don't know why you're so concerned. You're playing the jealous wife role perfectly."

I frown. "And you're playing the dismissive husband to a tee."

I hold his stare and the two of us stand there for a few moments, seething. Sebastian shakes his head after a few moments and walks away, leaving me in the empty hall.

*I*t's been a month since our fight. I walk out of the bathroom and collapse on the bed with a towel wrapped around me, just like I've always done back at my own apartment.

The past month has been mind-numbing to say the least.

The novelty of living in Sebastian's grand

home wore off a while ago, and our routine is always the same.

We show up to work together hand in hand, but as soon as no one is looking, Sebastian releases me like he can't bear to touch me a second longer.

I'm not going to lie, it kind of hurts my feelings.

And when we're not in public, Sebastian barely acknowledges my presence.

Weekends are the worst. Sebastian barricades himself in his office and doesn't show his head until Monday morning. I'm left to wander the gardens, with only Larry and the cardinals for company.

I haven't even met Sebastian's cook. She must do all of her cooking while we sleep or work, and a part of me wouldn't be surprised if that's how she prefers to work.

Sebastian is not exactly the friendliest boss to be around. If it weren't for the fact that I need to stay married to the guy, I wouldn't want anything to do with him either.

I don't know what I did to make him revert to his usual cold and grumpy self, but after our fight, he sent me a formal email to remind me of the rules in the contract I signed.

1. You must act professional at all times.
2. You will stay on your side of the house.
3. No emotional attachments to either parties of the contract.
4. No relationships with any persons inside or outside the marriage.
5. No intimate relations.

He's been distant ever since. If I thought he was grumpy and serious before we got married, he's much worse now.

Our first meeting with the immigration lawyer was surprisingly uneventful. It was one boring hour of talking about the immigration process and going through the paperwork, so I guess Sebastian was right. We didn't need to prepare for it.

But there's something about his mood swings that's unnerving. He was so warm and friendly in Vegas.

Once in a while, there are glimmers of the gentler side of him. Sometimes, I catch him looking my way as I'm pouring my cereal. But as soon as our eyes meet, he averts his gaze and looks at his phone. But in the millisecond before our eyes met, he had a soft smile on his lips.

I hate to admit it, but I miss him.

At least, before the marriage contract he talked to me like a human being. The party is drawing closer every day, and I'm nervous about whether he's going to be able to hide his obvious disdain for me.

I arch my stiff back with an irritated sigh and something black catches my eye.

I look up at the wall. There's a giant black spider crawling toward my pillow.

The reaction is instant and beyond my control. I leap off the bed and the towel on my head drops to the bed. I clutch the second towel around my body and let loose an earth-shattering shriek.

The creepy spider scuttles up the wall and stops by a picture frame. I hear hurried foot-steps and a loud bang.

Sebastian throws my bedroom door wide open and stands in the frame panting. All he has on is a pair of gray sweatpants that are sitting low and loose on his waist. His chest is heaving. Drops of sweat are clinging to his pectorals like diamonds. "What is it?" he demands, his eyes darting rapidly around the room.

I point at the spider on the wall and his eyes find it. "Are you serious?" he asks, incredulous.

I fist my towel and mumble incoherent apologies, mortified that he's found me like this. Without another word, Sebastian picks up the spider like it's no big deal and takes it outside.

I hold my breath until he's gone and exhale with relief. But he returns and gives me a hard look. "Listen, I warned you that you would be punished if you broke any of the rules."

*Is he for real?* "What rule have I broken, exactly?"

Sebastian crosses his arms across his broad chest and his nostrils flare. "Don't disturb my sleep for no good reason."

That is not a rule in the contract. His statement is so ridiculous; it's making my hands tremble.

"No good reason?" I repeat, my blood boiling. "I'm sorry my scream woke you up, but seeing a spider the size of my head crawling over me is reason enough..."

"It wasn't the size of your head," Sebastian says blandly. Amusement crosses his face for the briefest moment before he settles into a grimace again. "Fine, consider this a formal warning. Next time..."

"You'll what?" I give him a brazen look, forgetting that I'm only wearing a towel. But I will not, under any circumstances, be belittled by this man. Everyone knows spiders are scary. There's no need to be so mean.

Sebastian's breaths come out in puffs through his nose as he strides across the room and stops hardly a foot from me. I hold my breath, wondering what he's going to do next.

"You signed a contract," he says, his voice barely above a whisper. The words land on me like a slap. My face screws up in anger.

"I didn't sign up for *this*."

Sebastian takes a step back and his brows shoot upward. "What?"

I clutch my towel, my courage rising. I've wanted to give this man a piece of my mind for weeks but bottled it all up inside for the sake of his precious contract. Now everything is bubbling up to the surface and spilling over.

"I didn't sign up to be treated like a doormat. Or to get the silent treatment. I'm a person, you know? You can't just lock me up in a pretty prison, forbid me to have my own life, and then expect me to be happy."

Sebastian's expression is a cold grimace as he points to the open door. "Does that door look locked to you?" he asks, his chest heaving again. He doesn't wait for me to answer. "The contract is very clear. No relationships. No emotional attachments. One year of marriage in exchange for a million dollars." Then he drags a hand through his hair and starts to pace the room. "You know what I'll do? I'll add a clause. If you don't want to go through with this anymore, you can just go." He points at the door again and my stomach tightens.

When I don't say anything, he glowers at me.

"You're not a caged bird, Peyton. If you want to leave, leave. Nobody is stopping you. But just remember that if you stay, it's because you want to be here and *not* because I'm forcing you."

"You don't have to be so…" I blurt, but I hold my tongue at the sharp look Sebastian gives me.

"What? *Mean?*" He laughs darkly. "Let me make something very clear, Mrs. Rockwood." My breath hitches. "We are *not* lovers. We're not friends. We're not even co-workers. I'm your boss, and you're my PA. We've made an agreement that will earn you a massive pay raise."

I open and close my mouth silently as his eyes blaze.

"You're to play the role of my wife when we're in public. In private, you don't talk to me. You don't disturb me. *And* you don't disobey my rules. If you can't handle that, then there's the door. Take it. Rest assured, I won't be running after you."

Then he storms out of my room.

# SEBASTIAN

I pace, puffing air out of my nostrils until it burns. Ever since I got back to my room, I haven't been able to get to sleep. So, I gave up and decided to wear a hole in the carpet instead.

I'm not furious with Peyton. I'm furious with myself.

I knew she hated the silent treatment. I expected her to be miserable. But to stand up to me like that, cheeks flushed and damp hair splayed across her shoulders. She was daring, wild, and untamed.

Seeing her in just a towel, looking so raw and vulnerable, lit a fire in me. I didn't know what to do with it. I was sure her blood curdling scream was because there'd been a break in. Or a fire.

By the time I charged into her room and saw the situation, humiliation coursed through my veins at the fact that my protective instinct had taken over and I'd jumped into action without thinking.

Then she lashed out at me for mistreating her. I was right, she *isn't* locked up. But I can't deny that the way I've shut her out for the past month is unfair.

Being in the same room with her is agony. The more I've tried to keep her away, the more tension I've built up. She has become the forbidden fruit, and the more I deny myself, the more I lust for her.

I find myself lying awake in bed, fantasizing about a life where we can unwind, laugh, and actually get to know each other.

The touch of her hand in mine is addictive, sometimes I hold on to her a little longer than I should.

She's right. She didn't sign up to be mistreated. There has to be a way we can cohabit without getting into fights or undressing each other. But with Peyton, there doesn't seem to be an in-between.

Her sharp tongue cuts me in places I never knew I had. Her brazen, unapologetic expressions when she's yelling at me are both infuriating and arousing.

How am I supposed to keep this going for another eleven months?

I promise myself I'll ease off the silent treatment. I need to be polite. At the very least, treat her like I used to in the past, before the contract. We can keep our conversations on topics like the weather and work.

No confiding. No flirting. No jokes.

I can do this. I bite my fist, willing the tension in my body to ease.

Did I push her too far? What if she walks out and I never see her again?

The thought stabs me in the chest until my eyes water. I need to fix this.

I realize I'm not going to get any sleep tonight, so I get dressed and head out.

*T*he next morning, Peyton is deathly quiet on the ride to work. She barely tolerates me holding her hand as we walk into the office, and she's the first to pull out of my grip when we get to our floor. Before I can say anything, she darts to her desk and buries her head in work, leaving me to walk into my glass office with a heavy heart.

She's mad.

She's so angry her mood spreads like a dark cloud over the office. Some of the staff are muttering to each other and looking my way.

Are they gossiping about us? Probably theorizing about why Peyton has a look of thunder today. Maybe they can see the guilt written all over my face.

It's the first time in my life I've actually considered getting relationship advice. But I hold back the urge to call my therapist and pull out the little parcel in my jacket.

Whenever my grandfather did something to upset Grandma, he'd go out and buy her a goofy present to say sorry and cheer her up. One time, he came back with an Elvis Presley bobble head and a note saying, "I'll have a blue Christmas if you don't forgive me."

Another time, he bought her a tin whistle. I have no idea why he thought that was a good present, but it must have been an inside joke because when she opened it, she just laughed and laughed.

I hope I can get back on Peyton's good side with a gift.

Finding a store open in the middle of the night was tricky. I could only find gas station stores, and finding a suitable gift at a gas station was no mean feat.

I try to focus on work and simultaneously muster the courage to approach Peyton.

An opportunity presents itself at lunch when Eddie, the children's fiction editor, brings in donuts for his birthday. Everyone leaves their seats to congregate around his desk.

Everyone except Peyton and I.

I press the intercom. "Peyton. Can you come to my office for a moment?"

I see her face sour. But she slides her chair back and walks in with a clipboard to her chest.

"Yes, Mr. Rockwood?"

My stomach knots. "Don't call me that." I guess old habits die hard, but I'll never stop reminding her.

Her eyes flash at me, and the tension between us reaches new heights. I don't want to fight, so I sigh with defeat. "Fine," I say. Then I cross the office and close the door behind her. As I shut the blinds, I catch a few people looking our way. The staff will probably be gossiping about all the inappropriate reasons why I might be shutting the blinds. But the truth is I just want to have this conversation in private.

"What do you need?" Peyton asks. I sit on my desk and rest my hands on the edge.

"I need you to know that I feel guilty for the way I spoke to you last night," I say, softening my voice.

Peyton's shoulders drop a fraction of an inch. Clearly, she didn't expect to receive an apology.

That makes me feel worse.

"I was insensitive to your feelings. For that, I am sorry." I hold out the brown packet and offer it like a white flag.

To my relief, Peyton's expression softens as she takes it. "Oh. Well, I appreciate the apology..." But the she opens the packet and her eyes grow wide before she frowns at me. "Is this a joke?"

I cross my arms. "What?"

Peyton pulls out a replica wolf spider,

holding it by the leg with her thumb and index finger. "Why would you buy me this when you know I'm terrified of spiders?" She drops the model back in the packet and looks at me with a flushed face. Well, this was not the reaction I was hoping for.

I unfold my arms and clear my throat. "Exactly, you have an irrational fear of spiders. I heard that regular exposure is the cure."

"So you thought that I'd see this giant thing and be cured of my arachnophobia, did you?" Her eyes flash dangerously.

I roll my shoulders back. "I'm trying to apologize here. Can't you just be grateful?"

Peyton looks at the floor and shakes her head with a dark chuckle. "Chocolates would have worked just fine. Or heck, even a plain old apology. But this… This is sick."

I look at the packet in her hands and the blank expression on her face and my heart sinks.

"Is everything in order for the party this weekend?" I ask, switching the topic. Peyton flicks her hair back. The air cools between us. "It is. I've forwarded you the invoice from the caterers to look over."

I nod, relieved that we can at least be civil from now on. "Fine. Fine. You can go then."

Peyton heads for the door, but halts just before her hand reaches the handle. "Don't forget you've got an appointment with Tony tonight."

I look up from the floor. "Tony?"

"The immigration lawyer? For your biometric appointment." Peyton surveys me, and her eyes feel like a lie detector. I puff out my cheeks and swallow hard. She's talking about Tony the improv guy. I've been so wrapped up in work I forgot his name.

Lying is exhausting; so many details to keep track of. I nod along. "Right."

# PEYTON

Sebastian and I are sitting on the creaky old couch across from Tony Martins, the immigration lawyer. Tony is wearing the most garish yellow suit I've ever seen, and his tiny office smells like cigarette smoke. If it wasn't for the framed certificates on the walls, I'd never believe this guy was a lawyer.

He's almost bald on top, with a few wispy hairs combed over. I'm not sure who he's trying to convince. The one feature I can't get over is his bulbous nose and the large pimple on his left nostril.

The more I tell myself to look away, the harder I stare.

"The USCIS have received your application, and everything appears to be in order," Tony says, lacing his stubby fingers together. "I see you haven't attended your medical exam, yet?" He gives Sebastian a reproachful look. There's a bulge in Sebastian's jaw as he stares back.

"I have an appointment next week," he says curtly.

He's lying. The way his fingers tense is a tell. Plus, I know his schedule better than he does and there's nothing about a medical appointment for the next thirty days.

I make a mental note to remind him to book one.

"As long as you have your medical forms with you for the green card interview, that's fine," Tony adds. He coughs into his fist for several moments. Sebastian and I exchange looks.

There's a film of sweat on Sebastian's brow. Good grief, he's bad at this. At the rate we're going, he's going to crack under pressure during the interview and the office will discover this marriage is a sham.

Then what? I'll go to prison.

I take his hand. "So, how long will it take to get to the interview stage?" I ask.

Tony looks at Sebastian first, then clears his throat before he looks back at me.

"It's hard to say. There can be a number of delays. These things aren't quick."

This prompts Sebastian to start nodding. "We understand. Now, do you need to take my photo?" he asks, sitting more upright. It's nice to see that he doesn't flinch under my touch, but he won't look me in the eye. I guess he's still hurt by the way I took his apology.

Tony nods like a dog. "Yes, yes. Fingerprints and photos, yes." He turns to me, "Mrs. Rockwood, would you mind stepping out for a few moments?"

I hesitate and look at Sebastian, who finally looks at me. He gives me a nod. "I'll be right out."

"Erm... Sure, I'll be in the hall." I get up and leave the room, then I lean in to hear the muffled voices.

I can't make out the words, but Sebastian's voice is irritated. The two men engage in some sort of heated discussion for several minutes.

My brain is working overtime to figure out why something feels off.

I can't understand why Sebastian would be annoyed with the immigration lawyer. He hired him to help us. Getting a green card is what he wants, isn't it?

That feeling I had from the start comes back to me. He's hiding something, but I can't put my finger on what it is.

As I wait for Sebastian to come out, I look wistfully around the dark corridor. There are pictures of landscapes on the walls and the floor looks like it hasn't been mopped in years. I know Sebastian isn't short on cash, so I can't work out why he'd choose a place like this to do his visa paperwork. And why choose Tony? Tony, who can barely get through a sentence without hacking into his hand like the chain smoker he probably is.

Maybe he wants to keep things discreet. This side of the city is far away from anyone we'd know from work. Maybe he's worried that if the staff know he's going through an immigration process, someone might raise suspicion that our marriage is a fraud.

Yes. That must be it. I settle on that idea and stuff my hand in my bag, looking for my phone. My fingers curl around the brown packet instead. The spider model.

It's the first time Sebastian has bought me a gift, and it's the first gift I've received since my foster dad passed away.

A spider model.

I can't figure Sebastian out. He's warm and funny one moment, then he's cold and distant the next. Now he's buying me gifts. Terrible ones, but gifts all the same.

I smirk at the memory of Sebastian's face falling when he saw my reaction.

It's the worst apology present ever. But there's an old saying that it's the thought that counts.

I'll have to keep it in the packaging, but I've decided to keep the spider. In fact, I'll keep it with me at all times. Whenever Mr. Rockwood is being cold and harsh, I'll hold it and remember that he sucks at giving gifts, but he's not as cold-hearted as he makes out.

Above all, he isn't above apologies, and I appreciate that.

There's a sweet side of Sebastian just waiting to come out. I don't know why he insists on burying it. But I know that deep down, he cares about me.

The door opens and Sebastian forces a smile that doesn't reach his eyes. "All done," he says.

As we drive back to the house, Sebastian stays silent. He's trying to shut me out again.

But it's not going to work this time. The party is in two days, and I have the perfect plan to get Sebastian to show his true feelings.

# SEBASTIAN

*I*t's the night of the party, and I'm torn.

First of all, it's a relief to get this event over with. But I'd be more than happy to postpone the evening for another week or two. Or even indefinitely.

The main reason being that I've been able to get away with keeping PDA to a minimum so far. Behaving like a married couple at the office is easy; it's not appropriate to show affection or to be overly physical while at work.

But now that our colleagues are coming to our home, where there'll be alcohol, music, and dancing, they're going to expect a show.

As much as I love the idea of a bump and grind on the dancefloor, it would open up a can of worms that I'm just not ready to deal with.

There's a steady flow of cars pulling into the front of the house. I can see them from my office window. Peyton has outdone herself with the preparations. The trees are covered in fairy lights that twinkle like fireflies in between the leaves.

Men in suits are directing the traffic with light-up wands. They almost look like runway crew. And there are servers waiting by the front door to offer each guest a glass of champagne on arrival.

Peyton is a great PA. She keeps me organized, her paperwork is always done on time, and she can write in shorthand. But her special skill is apparently that the woman knows how to organize an event.

I've been in New York for eleven years and I've never thrown my own party. Without Peyton, I wouldn't know how.

I was invited to a few high society parties during my college years, but they were full of stuffy old rich men, who talked like they had sticks shoved up their butts, sharing fox hunting stories and bragging about the various ways they avoid paying taxes. Their Range Rovers and hunting dogs were so alien to me. I had no idea how to engage in conversation with them. The thought of standing around with people I can't relate to for hours on end is my idea of purgatory.

I have a glimmer of hope to hold on to tonight, though. If we're surrounded by literary-minded people, maybe there'll be some enlightening conversation to take part in.

But if I can get away with not having a party at all, I will always choose that option. I loathe people.

I can hear the band playing Moonlight Serenade outside and my tension eases. It's another one of Peyton's touches. She knows the classics calm me.

As my mind wanders back to her, a mixture of emotions swirl around in my stomach like snakes. We've shared several debates about our favorite authors.

She likes to list all of the reasons why Jane Eyre validates women's trust issues, and barrages me with verbal abuse over my belief that Pride and Prejudice is, quite frankly, ridiculous fiction.

Mr. Darcy is written as a moody, impolite man with no idea how to communicate with a woman.

How any female can read about such a man and swoon is beyond my comprehension. I could understand the appeal of the book if the ladies were falling for Mr. Bingley. He's kind, charming and smooth; far more likable.

I wince as I fix my tie. If I'm being honest, the real reason why I loathe Mr. Darcy is that I can relate to him on too many levels. Every time I think of him, I make a mental list of the things we have in common.

1. His general displeasure for making false pleasantries.
2. The intolerance for rude, disloyal family members.
3. The driving urge to do what is right and noble, at all costs.

My heart twinges. Am I doing the right thing by Peyton?

Yes. I'm protecting us both from heartache by keeping our arrangement professional. But if I were to take a leaf out of Mr. Bingley's book, I would at least be friendly with the woman. Maybe join her for dinner after work, or entertain her with jokes and good music. I'd actually take the time to get to know who she is when she's not my PA.

But I've been pushing her away. After I saw the fun, sassy side of her in Vegas, I realized I'm playing with fire. I'm not worried I won't get on with her. In fact, it's the opposite.

I liked the Vegas Peyton, and that scares me.

Now she's got her walls up, and I don't blame her. She keeps her tone professional at all times, and only takes my hand when its necessary. It's like holding a mannequin. Stiff. Immobile.

I sigh, full of conflicting emotions.

I feel guilty because I hurt her. I'm humiliated by the way she mocked my apology. Stressed over the fact that we still have a little over ten months to get through before this façade can end.

There's probably more I haven't unpacked yet, but my chest tightens at the thought of what I don't know.

I shrug on my suit jacket and tidy my hair, then roll my shoulders back.

I need to stop my brain from going into a frenzy. Overthinking is my superpower, but what use is it when I'm paralyzed by conflicting thoughts?

The most important thought tonight is the mission at hand. I'm hosting a celebration of my marriage to Peyton. Our guests need to buy the story; otherwise Peyton won't stop worrying about the repercussions. She doesn't stop talking about the immigration papers as it is, and I can't cope with her freaking out over the possibility of the staff derailing my fake application process.

So, for the next few hours, I'm going to have to behave like a doting husband.

Which means I'm going to have to touch her. A lot.

And I'll have to let her touch *me*.

There will probably be some kissing too, something we've been able to get away with not doing so far.

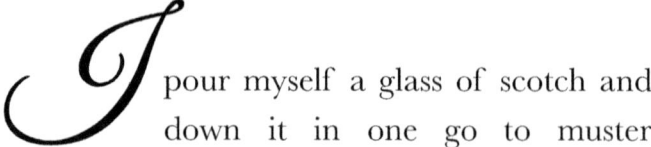 pour myself a glass of scotch and down it in one go to muster

courage. But I make a mental note to keep the drinking to a minimum tonight.

My frayed nerves are calling for alcohol, but I can't risk losing control. I might say something I shouldn't, or do something I'll regret.

My stomach lurches and I pour myself another glass.

I can't get through this night totally sober. I pour a final drink as a million worst case scenarios start to play in my mind.

A light knock on the door draws me back to the present.

"Come in," I call out. The door opens and a long satin skirt steps into view. My eyes dance over a shimmering ivory gown as Peyton walks into the office.

The dress is sitting snug on the swell of her hips and a dangerously high slit is showing off most of her left leg. I swallow and force my gaze upward, taking in the rest of her appearance in the process. Peyton's long dark hair is resting in loose waves on her bust, and the only things holding up the dress are two thin spaghetti straps.

My heart picks up speed and starts to

hammer my ribcage. I resist the urge to lick my lips.

She's drop dead gorgeous. This is going to make everything even more difficult.

Her pretty eyes blink at me when I finally meet her gaze, and the corners of her red lips curve upward for a flicker. But the smile fades so fast, I have to wonder if I imagined it.

"Are you ready? Everyone is asking for you," Peyton says, shaking her hair back from her shoulders. I glimpse her prominent collarbone for a second before I clear my throat with a nod. "What's the plan?" I ask.

"We'll make an entrance and greet everyone. Then you'll make a speech during drinks and hors d'oeuvres. We have a live band set up outside and…"

Peyton's voice fades as the sound of my heartbeat takes over. I swallow, suddenly unable to feel my fingers.

Peyton and I have been alone in a room countless times over the years, but I've never seen her like this.

She's never worn anything so revealing, and the way her hair flows in beach waves makes her look like a goddess. My overwhelming instinct is to drop to my knees and worship her.

I nod along and pretend I'm listening as she takes me through the agenda. When she's done, I offer my arm.

"Shall we?" I ask.

Peyton shuts her mouth and glances at the floor, then she gives me a look I can't read as she rests her hand in the crook of my arm. "We don't want to raise any suspicions tonight. There's rumors flying around that this isn't a real marriage, you know?"

That explains the odd look. She's worried I'm going to mess things up for her. That I won't be able to play the role convincingly.

I lift a brow. "Who's saying that?"

"Don't act surprised," Peyton shoots back. "You've not exactly tried to hide your dislike for me lately."

I clench my jaw. "Just because I don't have any feelings for you, doesn't mean I disdain you." There I go again, sounding like Mr. Darcy.

My words land on her like a slap and her cheeks turn red. "Well," she says gallantly. "Tonight we need to do something big to crush those rumors."

"Please don't tell me you want to re-enact the Dirty Dancing routine? Because let me stop you right there," I say, giving her a hard look. "I'm not Patrick Swayze."

Peyton laughs, so I guess she knows I'm not being serious.

We make our appearance and go through the motions. I rest my hand on the small of her back while we engage in small talk with a few guests.

Then we move on to the next group.

Watching Peyton laugh and crack jokes as we move from guest to guest; and seeing the way people react to her, is like watching a fireworks display on the Fourth of July. Her eyes are sparkling like her gown in the dim lights, and her smile practically lights up the whole garden.

Suddenly, the sound of glasses chinking sweeps like a wave across the whole garden.

"You know what that means," Lloyd from children's fiction says, his cheeks rosy from too much wine.

Everyone has loosened up, and now people are more confident to make demands.

"Give her a kiss!" someone shouts. That

prompts a chant of "kiss, kiss, kiss" that we can't ignore.

Peyton and I exchange looks and she gulps down her drink to buy us time.

Then, without giving me a second to react, Peyton grabs the back of my neck with both hands, stands on the tip of her toes and presses her body hard against mine, capturing my lips with hers.

# PEYTON

There's a single thought playing on repeat in my head.

*I'm kissing my boss. I'm kissing my boss. I'm kissing my boss.*

His mouth is hot and it tastes of hard liquor. His chest is tense against me, and a warmth spreads throughout my body like I've been wrapped up in a big security blanket.

There's romantic music playing in the background and the guests are cheering loudly. I can't tell if it's one or both, or something else, but something urges me to keep the kiss going.

Sebastian's big hands find my waist and he

lifts me up. The responding whistles and cheers almost make me laugh out loud.

We really look like a newly married couple now, totally in love. Our colleagues are buying the lie.

Heck, at this point in time, even *I'm* starting to believe it.

I wrap my arms around his shoulders and my hair falls over my face like a curtain, creating a barrier between us and the crowd. His nose and cheeks are touching my skin, and our breaths are hot and steamy in the cool, spring air.

I sneak a peek at him as we kiss. His eyes are closed. He slides his hands across my back and pulls me in even tighter. It's like he's never going to let me go. For a second, I think about the sea of people looking at us. I seem to be the one more in control of myself.

Then he sucks on my lip, and I forget about who's watching and just shut my eyes to fully enjoy the delicious moment.

I've learned something new today. Sebastian Rockwood is an *amazing* kisser. I make a mental note to add that to my statement for immigration.

When he's done with me and lowers me back to the ground, my lips are tingling.

I tuck my hair behind my ear with a nervous laugh, and our guests are raising their glasses in our direction.

"To Mr. and Mrs. Rockwood!" someone shouts from the back.

And just like that, everything is back to normal. The crowd breaks into circles of people chatting to each other.

Sebastian's hand is still holding mine. I glance at him with a shy smile.

Everything seems to be going according to plan tonight. And when I say plan, I mean the 'get Sebastian to show his true feelings' plan.

Step One: Put on a killer dress and act sexy. Check.

Sebastian gave me a credit card to pay for the party expenses. I figured a knockout designer gown was a necessary expense.

And oh boy, was that investment worth every cent. Seeing Sebastian's face light up when I walked into his office earlier sent a flurry of excited jitters through my body.

Step Two: Raise the stakes. Check.

I needed to make it clear that if we didn't play our roles perfectly tonight, his immigration application could be in jeopardy. I knew that would get him to man up and play his part.

Step Three: Kiss him in front of everyone.

There's no going back after that kiss. It was fantastic. Our eyes finally meet and I can't stop a grin.

The proverbial line between professionalism and something else altogether has been crossed. I'll never be able to look at him the same way again.

*S*ebastian squeezes my hand and doesn't let go as we sweep through the garden again, exchanging pleasantries with people.

Sebastian is being warm and charismatic, and he *won't* stop touching me. I like it. A lot.

When he does release my hand, it's only so he can rub my back, tangle his fingers in my hair or wrap his arm around my waist.

Every touch gives me butterflies. When I break away to grab a drink, his eyes never leave me. I feel the heat of his gaze on the back of my head as I talk to Joe from accounting. And now it's time for the final step in my plan.

Step Four: Make him jealous.

It seems cruel to do this, but the man has been hot and cold with me so many times, I need to make sure he's not going to shut me out again. I zone into Joe, trying not to stare at his quivering red mustache while he shares another bad joke.

"My ex-girlfriend dumped me because I used her toothbrush," he says. I blink and wait for the rest of the joke to land. Everyone knows 99.9% of the words out of Joe's mouth are not serious. He clears his throat. "I mean, it's a bit unreasonable when you consider how intimate you are with your partner, right? Besides, what else am I going to use to clean the toilet?"

And there it is.

I'd usually resist an eye-roll and offer a polite smile, but I'm on a mission to make Sebastian think I'm flirting. I toss my hair back, touch Joe's shoulder and give him a big girly laugh. "You're *so* funny, Joe!" I say as loud as I can.

I sneak a peek at Sebastian. He's still standing where I left him. He looks like he's about to crush his glass; the whites of his knuckles are on show.

I grin and turn back to Joe.

This guy is the biggest flirt at the office. He doesn't care about boundaries like whether the woman is married or not. In fact, rumor has it he'll start coming on to the men too when he's had enough to drink. It's happened at a couple of office parties.

I go along with his banter. Every time he says something insufferably offensive or pigheaded, I throw my head back and laugh like it's the funniest thing I've heard all year.

After a few minutes, Joe leans in, squeezes my arm and kisses me on the cheek. We've run out of things to talk about, so it's just Joe's way of excusing himself, but Sebastian's reaction is more than I could have hoped for.

Glass shatters and gasps erupt around the garden.

The next thing I know, Joe is pinned to the wall of the house and Sebastian is holding him up.

*Mayday. Mayday. Mayday.*

"Keep your hands off my wife," Sebastian growls. I'm not going to lie, that sounded pretty hot. Mr. I-Don't-Have-Feelings-For-You is jealous? I'll try not to tease him about this later.

The music stops and the sudden silence hangs heavy. Poor Joe is panting and Sebastian is taking long, slow breaths.

"S-S-Sorry Mr. Rockwood," Joe stammers. "We were just t-t-talking."

Sebastian leans in to him. "You don't talk to my wife. You don't touch her. Do you understand me? If I catch you even *looking* in her direction…"

Joe nods so fast I worry he's going to give himself whiplash.

I feel bad. This was interesting to see, but it wasn't the plan. No one was supposed to get hurt, or threatened.

Sebastian gives Joe one more stern glare before he drops him, turns around and sweeps me off the ground. "What are you doing?" I ask after I've recovered from the shock.

He bows his head to whisper in my ear. "What you asked of me. I'm acting like your husband."

*That is hot.*

I'm pretty sure I shouldn't be turned on by this toxic behavior, but the purely biological side of me doesn't know that. My boss is establishing his alpha dominance and I am here for it.

He carries me through the party and into the house. Absurdly, the guests are applauding. Somebody whistles. I almost want to laugh out loud. Sebastian steamrolled over my plan, but at least we gave the guests a good show. I can imagine the junior editors recounting the events with big eyes and lots of hand gestures. "He sucked her face off and then when he saw her talking to Joe, he dove right in there and slammed the guy against a wall."

No one can deny our relationship after witnessing that.

I'm proud. Sebastian played the role of possessive husband to a tee. Even *I'm* almost convinced it's real. Almost.

When he finally lowers me to the floor, I look around with a frown. "Sebastian, this isn't my room." He's kicking the door shut and yanking off his tie. "I know," he says, and strides toward a table with a canter and two crystal cut glasses.

"It's mine."

I stand frozen to the spot. The bed in the center of his room is massive. I try not to look at it. Twenty people could lay on it and there'd be room to spare.

I wonder if he ever gets lonely, sleeping in such a huge bed?

I shake myself quickly to force the thought out of my head.

*Don't go there, Peyton. You're getting carried away.*

Sebastian bends over and rests his palms on the table. I watch his shoulders rise and fall.

"What are we doing in your room?" I ask, walking up to him. I place my hand on his shoulder and he whips around to grab my wrist. He holds it up as his eyes bore into mine. "I've told you, Peyton. You belong to me. And I *don't* share my possessions."

His eyes fall to my mouth and my stomach flips again.

Is he going to kiss me again?

The flashback is sudden and electric. The velvet pressure of his lips. His hands on my body. His hard chest under mine. I lower my gaze to his mouth and lick my lips.

Great. Now *I'm* thinking about kissing him.

Slowly, Sebastian releases my wrist and

cups my face. Now his eyes are searching mine.

I don't know what he can see in them. Fear? Confusion? Annoyance?

Probably all three.

He's warm and charming one minute, then aggressive and brooding the next. I can't keep up.

But the overwhelming emotion I have inside of me right now is a deep longing to break down the walls around him. I want him to show me the sweet side of him I know is buried inside.

Is it so terrible to want my husband of convenience to let me in?

I blink up at him and try to read his eyes. They're so dark. It's like looking into the forest at night and trying to see the leaves.

I swallow. He's just hovering. His hands are still cupping my face and I'm trapped in his gaze.

"I hate seeing you with another man," he says finally.

The words come out like a groan. As though saying them caused him great pain.

The confession soothes me and I feel a rush of warmth for him.

This man. This mysterious beast of a man who knows how to keep a woman on her toes. I reckon it'll take me a lifetime to truly understand the workings of his mind.

If this arrangement is just business and he truly only sees me as his PA, then why does he want to destroy anyone who might even look at me?

"I was only talking to Joe. You know he's harmless."

Sebastian drops his hands and snorts.

"You say you're so worried about people thinking that our relationship isn't real. Yet you go flirting with other guys at our party. Peyton, I can't figure you out."

I chew my lip. He's right. "I didn't think about it like that."

Sebastian shrugs off his jacket and tosses it to the bed, then he rolls up his shirt sleeves. I stand mute and immobile. I wonder how he'd react if I traced a finger along those bulging veins on his arm? Would he pull away or would he melt?

He begins to unbutton his shirt. I suck in a breath and look away, out at the fairy lit gardens.

"Are you not going back out to the party?" I ask.

Sebastian ruffles his hair with a sigh. The top three buttons of his shirt are undone now and I catch a glimpse of his chest. But I avert my eyes again when he catches me staring. "We've done our job. No one cares to see us anymore. They won't even notice we're gone."

I fiddle with my silver bracelet and stare at the carpet while Sebastian busies himself with the drinks. Then I remember his words earlier and a flush of heat rises to my face. I have a question. I gather the courage to ask it. "You said you were going to make it clear that you don't share. What do you mean by that?"

Sebastian turns and offers me a drink but I shake my head. I'm jittery enough with just one glass of wine in my system. I don't need any more alcohol.

Sebastian cocks a brow at my pass and puts the two glasses on the table. It's the first time I've seen him resist a drink.

"I don't want anyone at the office getting any ideas," he says, dragging a thumb across his bottom lip. I follow the stroke of his finger like a woman in a trance.

The kiss is still fresh in my mind. Coupled with the fact that my boss just carried me into his room, I'm on fire.

"Ideas?" I ask, forcing my brain to think about something other than kissing him again.

Sebastian smirks. "Come on. Don't play dumb. You're hands down the sexiest woman here tonight. And I'll wager that there are at least twenty men who would make a move if they thought they could get away with it."

My cheeks are flaming now. "Sebastian, it's a party to celebrate our *marriage*. How can you possibly think…"

"How can you be so naive?" Sebastian shoots back.

Sebastian bites his fist for a second. "Even *I'm* struggling to resist…"

I look at him in surprise. "Resist what?" I ask.

Sebastian doesn't answer, he just stares at me through hooded eyes.

Oh my gosh.

My heart skips a beat and I break out into a nervous sweat.

I can't decide whether to make a run for it or stay and see where this goes.

At least tonight I'm not wearing silly character underwear.

There's an internal battle going on inside of Sebastian's head. I can tell by the bulge in his jaw and the way his eyes keep shifting from side to side. Scenarios start to play out in my head.

I see him charge forward and wrap me up in his arms. He kisses every inch of my exposed skin and then grabs my neck and whispers something toxic like, "You're mine and I'll make sure no one else can ever have you."

I shiver on the inside and suppress a smile.

I shouldn't be having these fantasies about my boss. Sure, we're married. Sure, we shared a kiss as hot as fire. But the contract was very clear, and it's still very real.

No intimacy. No feelings. No *actual* relationship.

We stand there for a few minutes, just staring at each other.

The tension in the room is building to a pitch.

"You need to leave," Sebastian says suddenly, cutting into my visions of us making out right here in the middle of his room. I blink several times to take in his words.

"What?"

Sebastian takes a single step forward and I see that his hands are balled into tight fists.

"Go. Right now. Get out of here. Before I..."

"Before you what?" I step forward. I've had enough of this cat and mouse game.

To my delight, he takes a step back. For the first time, I've got the upper hand.

A flash of uncertainty crosses Sebastian's face before he scowls at me again. He takes a huge breath. "Before I do something we'll both regret," he finishes. He runs his eyes over the length of my body and I suddenly have goosebumps.

"Something like...?" I take another step forward. My left thigh is now exposed, thanks to the dramatic split in my gown. Sebastian's eyes flicker to my leg but return quickly to my face. Seeing him react this way sends a rush of tingles all over me. The thought that my grumpy boss, the man who is always ready to assert his dominance, is suddenly looking more like prey than predator, is wildly exciting.

I never knew I could have this effect on him. Or on anyone for that matter. He scratches the back of his neck and makes a noise like a dying lion. No one is watching us here. We're in his room, totally alone. This can't be an act. But is it really so painful for him to resist me? *He* was the one who wrote up that stupid contract, after all. Is this why he's been shutting me out?

I make the bold decision to walk right up to him, and my body is now mere inches away from his. A flood of heat rushes over me as I look him square in the eye. If I heave my chest, our bodies will touch. So, I make sure to keep my breaths shallow as I stare him down, testing him.

"Tell me what you want to do to me," I demand.

He reaches for my hair and tangles his fingers in a lock of it. Then he rolls his bottom lip inward and licks it. I hold still, resisting the urge to shiver with delight at his touch. I don't want him to know the effect he has on me. Not yet.

He searches my eyes with his again. "Oh,

if you only knew the things I want to do to you. With you. For you."

"What things? Tell me."

Sebastian pulls my hair away from my neck and grazes his cheek against mine. His hand finds the small of my back. But then he stiffens, drops his hand, and pulls back. "No. You need to leave."

Every atom in my body is buzzing and my brain can't keep up with the situation.

"Why?" I almost yell at him. He walks past me and begins to pace the room.

"Because of the contract. My promise. I'm a man of my word, Peyton."

Before I can react, Sebastian strides to the door and opens it wide for me. "Go and tell everyone the party is over. Then go back to your room."

His instructions irritate me. There he goes again, giving me orders. I guess old habits die hard after ten years. As though he's reading my mind, he gives me a stern look.

"I'm still your boss."

# SEBASTIAN

I swear the ice-cold water must be steaming off my back. I hunch over with my hand pressed against the tile walls of my shower stall and just let the water's hard pressure help me clear my mind.

Peyton is tempting me. Dangling herself like a juicy steak in front of a tiger.

And oh, how badly I want to pounce and get a taste.

I watch the water coming off me swirl around the drain. I need to calm down.

The effect she has on me is like nothing I've ever known. She's infuriating and intoxicating all at the same time.

I want to throw her on the bed to stop her

from talking, and then I want to keep her quiet with my lips. I'd go on kissing her until the only sounds coming from her mouth are moans.

The attraction I have to her is electrifying, and it's ramped up several notches since our kiss.

My body was ablaze with need. I wanted to worship every part of her body and soul.

I will never forget the way her body fit so perfectly in my arms. Or the little noises she made when I gave her hair a tug.

I finally step out of the shower and wrap a towel around my waist before I march to the window. The gardens are empty but for the cleaning staff removing all evidence that there was ever a party.

The birds are chirping again, having been dead silent during the music and dancing.

Larry the parrot is uncharacteristically quiet today. He must still be overwhelmed by all of the people and the chaos of the party. I can relate.

I thought I was coping with the party pretty well, considering I don't enjoy being around people. Until the kiss.

From that moment, all my senses came alive.

My blood effervesced with alcohol and sugar. My ears were ringing with the jumbled sounds of classical music, laughter, and glasses chinking. Every time I touched Peyton, it set off a chain reaction of tiny shocks. The sensation was addictive; I couldn't keep my hands off her.

Then she started talking to Joe. Laughing at his lame dad jokes, touching his arm, and then his shoulder. When he kissed her, it was like someone set off a bomb in my head. All I could see was red.

I know I overreacted. I should have been more diplomatic. I half expect a resignation on my desk Monday morning.

On the bright side, Peyton isn't likely to waste any more time worrying what the people at the office think about our marriage. And I highly doubt that anyone else will try to make a move on her.

So it's a win-win.

I wish I had more restraint. If I can find a way to keep those sudden urges at bay, maybe I can spend more time with her. I bite my lip as the things I imagine doing with her flash

through my mind's eye. Us reading on the
couch on lazy Sunday mornings. The two of
us walking in the gardens, listening to the
wind ruffling the leaves of the trees.

Those thoughts calm me.

Now that everyone is gone and I'm out of
the shower, I'm clear enough in my mind to
admit that, once again, I was a jerk to Peyton.

It's incredibly frustrating, but the woman
makes me want to be a better man.

I was trying to respect our agreement, but
I snapped.

I pull on a pair of sweatpants and drag the
towel through my damp hair, trying to decide
whether to go and apologize to her or just
leave it until morning.

It's the weekend; I usually hole myself up
in the office and work. And when I say work, I
mean avoid Peyton and wrestle with my
thoughts.

The woman has invaded my brain. I'm
wracked with guilt.

I should know better. Words cut deeper
than knives. I need to pay more attention to
what I say to her and how I behave.

In truth, I want to fall to my knees and
apologize right now; grovel and beg for her

forgiveness. Tell her that I'm not just her boss, I'm her husband. Her servant. I'll do anything to keep her safe, to make her laugh. Yes, she is mine. But the raw fact is that she is the true captor in this situation.

She has my heart clamped in her hands and I'm completely at her mercy.

Before I can talk myself out of it, I march out of my room and head for her side of the house. I know if I don't at least apologize, I won't sleep a wink.

When I reach her room, I hear sobbing.

I push the door open and call out her name.

The room is empty and dark but for the soft glow coming from under the bathroom door. I should probably leave, but a voice that sounds like Peyton's says, "Alexa, all lights on."

The room is instantly flooded with lights. Larry is perched proudly in the ornate bird cage by the window. He cocks his head and gives me a shrewd look with one eye.

I guess Peyton didn't want her parrot outside during all the commotion.

Another loud sob interrupts my thoughts and I turn my attention to the bathroom.

"Peyton?"

I knock and the door squeals open. A mist of hot vapor covers me.

The crying stops for a moment and there's a sniff. When I peer through the steam, I see Peyton hugging her knees on the floor of the shower stall. She's still wearing her dinner gown.

When she looks up at me, her face is blotchy and lined by two black streaks of mascara. She's soaked to the bone.

All of my instincts kick in. My brain is suddenly working overtime, trying to piece together what has happened to break her this way.

"Who did this to you?" I growl. "Give me a name and I'll make sure they never hurt you again."

I half expect her to say Joe. I'll kill him if he did something to her. I'll rip him limb from limb and...

"It wasn't Joe," Peyton mutters, reading my mind.

I grab a big towel, reach through the spray and haul Peyton out of the stall by her shoulders. I put the towel around her as gently as I can and try to understand, get some sense out of her. "Tell me then. Who did this?" I press.

Peyton blinks water out of her lashes and stares at me with a look of total devastation. "You did."

The words go straight to my heart and shatter it on impact.

# PEYTON

The thing about being a woman is, you can bottle up your emotions for a really long time and think you're being a total girl boss at life, then one seemingly insignificant thing will destroy the dam and all hell breaks loose.

All it took to break me were four little words.

*I'm still your boss.*

It wouldn't ordinarily have had much of an impact on me. It's not the first time Sebastian has snapped something like that at me, or put me right back in my place as sharply as he can manage. Heck, he's been downright frigid.

But for some reason, those words crushed me that night.

I don't know if it's because I had all this built-up anticipation of what he might do to me. Maybe getting such an abrupt reminder of the situation was what did it.

After I announced the party was over and made sure all the guests had left the premises, I signed forms and gave instructions to the clean-up staff. Then as soon as I got to my room, I cracked.

The past few months have been like something out of a Twilight movie written and directed by Adam Sandler; equal parts sexual tension and angst, with outrageously cringe moments.

When Sebastian came running into the bathroom and found me a hot mess on the bathroom floor, I didn't even flinch. Now I can't look him in the eye, I'm so mortified.

He kept sucking all of the energy out of me with his mood swings. It's like somebody had control over my life and was pulling petals off a daisy; "He wants me, he loathes me."

I wish I knew what was going on inside his head when he saw me like that. He kept his thoughts to himself and just carried me out of the bathroom like I was an invalid.

Anyway, it's been four months since that night and I've been doing all the avoiding.

I keep my head down, do my work, and make excuses to sit as far away from him as possible during meetings.

He's tried to start friendly conversation in the car a few times, but my one-word answers don't leave any room for that. He gave up trying eventually.

So, here we are. We're halfway through the 365 days I signed up to be Mrs. Rockwood. Another six months to go.

Thankfully, work has been enough to keep us on our toes during the week and through the weekends. We've had six book launch events, multiple signings, and fourteen new authors. It's been a boatload of leg and paperwork. I'm starting to suspect Sebastian is piling on the work to make time go by faster.

I'm not complaining, though. The sooner this year is over, the sooner I'll be riding off into the sunset with my freedom and a million bucks.

I'm sitting in Elle's Kitchen, surrounded by happy families and powerful smells of sugary goodness. None of it is doing anything to lift my mood.

I haven't been back since the time Sebastian brought me here, but I came in for a strawberry milkshake and donut craving. Ever since my appetite became a ravenous beast, I've gained a few pounds. Okay, maybe more than a few. I'm up at least one dress size.

"Peyton, it's nice to see you again!" I hear Elle call. She sounds like there are no problems in the world. And she's carting an enormous bump in front of her.

I'm impressed she remembered my name. She must have taken one of those online courses that teach you how to remember stuff like a robot.

Elle Masters moves through her store on autopilot. Her face is sunny and bright, and she's pulled her blonde hair back into a bouncy ponytail. Heck, even her glossy hair looks happy.

She seems to be friends with everyone. And on paper, I feel like *we* should be friends. Maybe even besties.

But there's just something about Elle that grates on me. Every time I look at her, I see perfection and happiness. She has it all.

The billionaire husband who adores her, her mom's bakery, the love of everyone in New York. Pretty soon, even her giant bump will turn into another amazing part of her life; a picture-perfect baby to complete her picture-perfect life.

I grit my teeth and rise, ready to leave the untouched milkshake on the table.

Now I get it.

The reason why I'm triggered every time I see Elle Masters is because she symbolizes everything I never had.

A caring mom, a rich, loving husband. Friends... Not to mention a thriving business.

And what do I have? *Who* do I have?

I have Larry, my parrot. And the promise of $1M as long as I stick to the terms of a stifling contract and stay married to my insufferable boss for another six months.

My life is depressing.

But I guess the forecast is that things will get better. I've come this far by daydreaming about what I'm going to spend all that money on.

The sensible thing to do would be to invest in stocks or property... Something like that.

Maybe I'll travel the States on a motorbike with Larry's cage tied to the back. Or buy a ranch in Texas and hire buff men to work on it while I sip Piña Coladas on the porch and watch them sweat it out. Shirts won't be part of the uniform.

Both scenarios are dumb. I'd never do those things. I'm not sure I hate the idea of watching buff shirtless men on a ranch for the rest of my life, though.

One thing is certain, I'm handing in my resignation and leaving this city as soon as I can.

I'm still humiliated by the way things turned out on the night of that party.

Kissing Sebastian like that, only to get pushed away, really hurt me. Then for him to find me crying in the shower like a girl who just got dumped at prom was the cherry on the top of a very bitter cake.

Now, when Sebastian looks at me, he's not cold or distant. It's worse.

I see pity.

I thought the silent treatment was horrible, but this is definitely more awkward.

Honestly, I'll take cold and distant Sebastian any day.

My stomach is in knots when I leave the bakery. Outside the store, I hug myself. Strong gusts of wind throw themselves at me as I head for the subway.

This year has been nothing but gray skies and thunderstorms. The wettest spring on record led to the coldest summer on record. I wish mother nature would get her act together and give us a blast of sunshine for a couple of days. As we enter September and get ever closer to my thirty-fourth birthday, I can only hope we get a reprieve from this depressing weather. Even if it's just for a day.

Some people say the weather reflects our mood. Maybe my hidden super power is that the elements are affected by the way I feel.

If that's true, the world may never have a sunny day again.

"Where have you been? Mr. Rockwood has been asking for you," is the receptionist's greeting as I walk into the office building. Not *Hello. How are you?*

I smother my irritation. The poor girl is probably just stressed out because we have that big meeting today. This is when every senior editor from every department pitches the story they want to publish to Sebastian. It's going to be long and laborious, and tensions are high all round.

"I'm heading up now. Is everyone gathered in the conference room already?"

The phone rings and the receptionist answers the call without another look my way. I shake my head and walk away "She's on her way up, Mr. Rockwood," I hear her say.

The conference room is packed. I'm sure we're breaking several health and safety guidelines.

I squeeze into the corner and perch on the last vacant seat directly underneath an AC vent. Lucky me. The steady blast of cold air gives me instant goosebumps. Now I'm kicking myself for not bringing a sweater. I swear it'll be just my luck if I end up getting the flu.

"Now that everyone is here, let's get started, shall we?" Sebastian says after a brief glance my way. There's a stack of folders on the table in front of him.

I scribble furiously, taking down the minutes while senior editors take turns pitching. My brain should be on autopilot, but we might as well call today Upside Down Day because I'm fully tuned in when Charlie, the women's fiction senior editor, starts to pitch a story that might as well be my back story. It's like I've jumped into an alternate reality and this guy is pitching my life to Sebastian and everyone else at the office.

"So, this one is about a young woman named Zoe. She grew up in foster care, never knew her birth parents. She moves into the city to reinvent herself after years of bullying, but instead of landing partner in a law firm like she planned, she's a personal assistant to the richest bachelor in the state."

My neck almost snaps as I look up at Charlie in horror.

Is this a joke? Who wrote this? I start to click my pen in a nervous tic. A few heads turn to look at me.

I force my attention back to my notebook. I wish that I had my laptop to hide my face behind, I'm sure it's turning red. But I stopped taking notes on my laptop a while ago.

I swallow and try to write down the rest of the pitch.

"She's awkward and kind of a loner, but she's got spunk, you know? She realizes she's in her mid-thirties and enough is enough. So she decides to stop being a loser and takes off on a mission to make something of herself..."

I can't feel my hands. The pen is frozen on my notepad and there's an ice-cold sensation sweeping up my arms and chest.

"...of course, then she makes a succession of foolish choices. Further alienating herself from others..."

My ears are ringing now. I can no longer hear Charlie. There's an eerie, high-pitched squealing in my ears; everything else is a faint rumble in the background.

My breaths are coming fast and shallow. The room begins to spin.

*Oh, no. Please not now. Please not now.*

The last time I had an anxiety attack this severe was in high school, during exams. I blacked out fifteen minutes to the end of the paper and they had to reschedule it. I made a lot of enemies that day.

I will myself to take long, deep breaths, but the iciness is spreading to my neck and it's like a pair of hands are closing their grip on my jugular.

"I can't breathe," I whisper, clutching my throat.

There's sudden commotion. I slide out of my chair and fall to my knees on the floor.

The next thing I know, people are on their feet and marching out of the room fast.

I don't care. I no longer care what anyone thinks. Right now, all that exists is pure panic. My body is refusing to let me breathe. Hot tears leak out of my eyes and I blink up to see Sebastian closing the door.

It's just us now. He closes the blinds and shrugs off his jacket.

Maybe he'll fire me right here and now. Probably rip up the contract too. That'll be six months of my life I'll never get back. And for nothing.

I'll end up on the streets, walking past Elle's Kitchen just to get a waft of the glorious smell. A reminder of what my life used to be like.

I won't be able to afford Larry's bird feed. I'll have to set him free.

*Don't pass out. Don't pass out. Don't pass out.*

I repeat the words like a chant in my head.

Sebastian's shiny black shoes walk across the polished floor and stop in front of my knees. Then Sebastian crouches and his worried face comes into view.

I look at him and try not to break into sobs as I wait for the fatal blow.

*Go on, fire me. I dare you.*

Sebastian puts his arms around me and pulls me in for a tight hug. My butt plops onto his lap and my body is totally cocooned in his arms and chest. I can hear his heartbeat thumping against my ear. The ringing in my ears starts to fade.

He brushes my hair away from my face and whispers into my ear. "You're okay. I've got you. You're going to be okay."

Then he rocks me back and forth, squeezing me. Tears roll down my cheeks. I bury my face in his chest and inhale his woody scent.

"I won't let anything bad happen to you. I promise," he says.

He kisses me on the top of my head, and like magic, a sense of calm washes over me. It starts at my head and rolls down my neck, releasing the tension in my chest and my arms. My hands begin to tingle.

*This* is what I needed that night when he found me in the shower, and I didn't even know I needed it at the time.

I needed this hug.

If he hadn't bolted from my room and left

me alone to compose myself, things might have been different.

If he had stayed and comforted me, we could have started something. Four months ago.

*Four months*, I repeat in my head.

Sebastian strokes my hair and rubs my back and it's like he's wiping away all of the hurt that accumulated over that time.

I wriggle against his chest, trying to make the most of this moment before he lets me go. He holds me even tighter.

Then he whispers something into my hair and it's so quiet, I'm not sure if I imagined it.

"I promise I'll never, ever let you go again."

# SEBASTIAN

I wait patiently for Peyton's breathing to return to normal. Her tears are soaking my shirt, but I don't care. I should drown in her tears. I deserve it.

The nightmare I've put her through this year is the worst thing I've ever done. I'll spend the rest of my life making it up to her.

Once Peyton is calm, I pull back to look at her face and wipe the tears from her eyes.

"Will you let me take you home?" I ask.

She blinks several times as though I've just spoken in a foreign language.

"You're asking?" she asks in apparent disbelief.

Her reaction drives another dagger into

my chest. All this time, I've called the shots and expected her to do whatever I say.

It's the kind of boss I've always been. The man with an iron fist. It's kept things clean and practical, and I have to admit it gets the job done.

But things are so complicated with Peyton.

I didn't consider the effects being in a marriage would have on us both. Emotionally. Physically. Mentally.

It feels wrong now to boss her around. I can't work out when exactly things changed on that front, but I see it clear as day.

"I don't want to do anything that makes you uncomfortable," I tell her. "If you're agreeable, I want to take you home and call a doctor."

Peyton shakes her head and sniffs. "No," she says, but then she scrunches up her face. "I mean, yes. I want to go home. But I don't need to see a doctor. It was just an anxiety attack."

It wasn't just an anxiety attack, not from where I was standing. It was much more. But I don't argue.

With her consent, I pick her up in my arms

and she clasps her hands behind my neck. I walk her out of the conference room and ignore the sea of faces aimed in our direction, but my ears don't miss the hushed voices and excited chatter. I guess to them this looks like a worried husband carrying his wife out of the office.

When in actual fact, I'm not worried. I'm angry.

Angry with myself for letting things drag on this long. I have spent countless nights pacing my room, trying to think of something I can do to apologize to Peyton. But she hated the last attempt so much, I wanted to get it right this time.

Chocolates didn't feel right.

The longer I spent thinking about it, the worse it got. Peyton wouldn't engage in conversation more than a few words at a time, then she wouldn't even look at me.

I was worried that she was going to leave. And I wouldn't have blamed her if she did.

I'm glad she didn't, and I'm now on a mission to bring this ship around. From now on, I'm going to be everything she needs me to be.

As soon as we're back home, I settle

Peyton on the couch in the living room and light a fire to warm her up.

She accepts coffee and a fleece blanket, and she keeps giving me furtive looks, but she stays silent.

I'm pretending I'm busy with work on my laptop, but I can't stop looking at her either.

I want to ask what happened back at the office, but only when I'm sure she wants to talk about it.

Her soft brown hair falls over her shoulders, framing her pretty face. Her skin is blotchy and her lips are swollen, but she's the cutest I've ever seen her.

Finally, after some time has passed, she speaks.

"Do you want to know something funny?" she asks. The question takes me aback. I nod. Peyton snorts, looking darkly into the fire.

"That book Charlie was pitching today…" She drags her gaze to meet mine. "It sounded a lot like someone had written a book about my life."

Before I can hold it back, my face twists into a confused frown. "I suppose there were a few similarities. The woman working as a PA, but…"

Peyton shuts her eyes with a sigh and puts her coffee down. "I was a foster kid, too."

"Ah."

It's all I can say.

She wants to say more, but there's a pained expression in her eyes and I can see just the little she's said has taken a lot out of her.

I join her on the couch and put one arm around her shoulders. To my relief, she rests her head on my chest. She fits so comfortably in my arms. I smooth out her hair and inhale her berry-scented shampoo.

"Don't worry," I say, in a resolute tone. "That book won't get published. In fact, I'll fire Charlie for pitching it."

Peyton lifts her head to study my face, perhaps looking for a sign that I'm joking.

When she sees that I'm absolutely serious, she taps me on the arm. "You can't do that."

She looks away and breaks into a light laugh. It's the most pleasant sound I've heard in a long time.

"But I appreciate the thought, though," she adds with a smirk.

We stare into each other's eyes for a long time, and a strong emotion rises in my chest. I rest my knuckle under her chin. "I know this is rather unconventional," I begin. Peyton's neat brows twitch toward each other. If I don't say what's in my head now, the moment will pass and who knows what will happen?

"But I would like to take you on some dates and get to know you better. Would you be agreeable if I asked you out?"

Peyton's blotchy face goes red and she breaks out into a grin.

"I thought you'd never ask."

# PEYTON

*I*t's my birthday.

I hate birthdays. Mine have been nothing but disappointments year after year. This year is different though. I'm not spending it alone, for one thing.

I'm in a sort-of relationship with a guy who sucks at gift-giving, but he makes up for it in other ways.

He woke me up with a bouquet of flowers. "I'm not going to sing," he said, while he put the flowers in a vase and set them on my nightstand. "Because I'm pretty sure I'm tone deaf and you don't want to hear that."

I chuckled and yanked the covers over me.

It's not the first time Sebastian has come into my room while I'm in bed, but it still makes me nervous.

Now he's sitting at the bottom of the bed with his legs stretched out and crossed at the ankles.

"I've thought long and hard about your gift," he tells me.

I point to the flowers. "Aren't they my gift?"

Sebastian shakes his head and chuckles to himself. "No. I mean, your main gift."

My stomach flips. This is already the most exciting birthday I've ever had.

"Okay, I'm listening."

Sebastian reclines back and looks up at the ceiling. He's wearing a casual shirt with the sleeves rolled up. Whenever he's dressed this way, I find myself staring at all the veins bulging from his muscular arms. He looks at me again. "I'm giving you a yes day."

"A yes day?" I repeat, confused.

Sebastian is grinning now.

"Ask for anything today and I'll say yes."

My stomach does a somersault. "Anything?"

Sebastian nods. "Yes."

I tap my leg in thought. "So, if I asked you to take me on a private helicopter ride to the Grand Canyon…?"

"I can arrange that."

I almost squeal with excitement. Today is going to be amazing.

*T*he first thing I ask Sebastian for is a day off work. "I already took the liberty of clearing our calendars last night and telling the office we won't be in today," he confesses. I gasp.

Sebastian hasn't taken a day off in… Forever.

The next thing on my list is a trip to the spa. Without hesitation, Sebastian takes me to some fancy club.

He offers me a round of golf, but whacking tiny balls with sticks just isn't my kind of thing. We get a couple's massage instead.

When we're done, he sits on the edge of

the massage bed in nothing but the white fluffy towel he wrapped around his waist. His body is oiled up from the massage, and every bulging muscle is dewy.

"What next, birthday girl?" he asks, sweeping a hand through his hair. I take a sip of my champagne. The bubbles might have just gone straight to my head.

"I want to see a Broadway show. I've lived in the city all these years and I've never been to one."

Sebastian grins. "Any particular preference?"

I shake my head. I've never stepped foot in a theater before. Just the thrill of having that experience is enough.

Sebastian makes a few calls, and after an impromptu trip to a designer store, where he buys me a new dress and heels, we walk arm in arm into a theater.

Pretending to be Sebastian's wife is easy now. My hand rests on the crook of his arm as we climb the carpeted stairs and Sebastian takes us to a private box.

I stare wide-eyed at the stage, riveted by the orchestral music.

Sebastian finds my hand halfway through and holds it on his knee for over an hour. Every time there's a loud noise that makes me jump, he squeezes. A gentle reminder that he's here for me.

After the show, he takes me to the Ritz for a dinner reservation. I keep smiling at him. He's wearing a sharply tailored suit, and he looks so refined while we eat our food. None of this feels real.

"Is there anything else you want to ask?" he says while he helps me into a cab.

Today has been like something from a fairy tale. Sebastian has treated me like a princess throughout, and I honestly can't think of anything else to top it off with. I wonder if I can use my 'yes day' to take off another layer and get to know him better.

"Tell me what your biggest fear is," I ask.

Sebastian takes his time to answer. In fact, he doesn't say a word until we roll up to the house.

"I know..." he says, as though he's been thinking about it this whole time and he's been struck by a sudden revelation. But he doesn't finish his sentence. Not yet.

He pays the driver and helps me into the house.

We halt in the entry way, and my glittery dress shimmers under the ceiling light. I'm nervous now, but looking at Sebastian makes me all warm and fuzzy.

Sebastian takes off his jacket and unbuttons the top of his shirt. "My greatest fear…" he says slowly. I love his thinking face.

That line between his brows deepens and he pouts a little.

We haven't kissed since the party. Even though Sebastian has been taking me out on dates for the past fortnight, we've kept things formal.

I guess there's a worry that going in too deep might mess up the good thing we've got going. Heaven knows we've experienced several swings from great to disaster.

Things feel different, though. I have no worries or inhibitions. All I want to know is if he'll kiss me back if I make a move.

*S*ebastian reaches for my hair and brushes it past my shoulder. Then he rubs his thumb along my jaw and curls his fingers around my neck. I shudder under this touch.

I find his eyes again and he looks so serious now. "I fear rejection," he says.

It's not the reply I expected. I mean, I know he's not afraid of spiders. But I expected something funny, like clowns or unpaid taxes. Rejection isn't anything to laugh about. I blink quickly as the words settle in my mind.

Rejection. Now everything makes sense. Why he keeps everyone at arm's length. Why he tends to be grumpy and cold. Why he's so quick to reject others.

He's protecting himself.

"Why rejection?"

His Adam's apple bobs.

"Do I have to answer that? I know I said today is yes day but…"

There's trouble in his eyes. "No. You don't need to," I assure him. Clearly, something happened to him in his past that he's not ready to talk about. Plus, being this close to him, with his hand on my neck and his other hand on my waist, is quickly making it hard for me to even want to keep talking.

"We still have a couple of hours left. What

else do you want for your birthday?" he whispers.

I look up at him through my lashes. My hands work of their own accord and wrap themselves around his neck. I rise up on tip-toes to brush my lips over his.

"I want you," I whisper against his mouth. Sebastian's grip on me stiffens, but he doesn't lurch away. I feel him settle instead. Then he nuzzles my nose and presses his forehead against mine.

"What are you asking me?" he whispers back.

We don't let go of each other as I lead us to my room. Once inside, I kick off my heels. Sebastian finally releases me when I turn my back to him. "Will you unzip my dress?"

Sebastian takes the zipper in one hand and grazes his knuckle over every inch of my spine as he drags the zipper down to my lower back.

"Thank you," I whisper when he's done.

Sebastian looks at me and his eyes are dark with desire. I bet if I place my palm against his chest, I'll feel his heart racing.

Mine is racing too.

"I have one last request," I say, surprised at how bold I sound when I'm quivering on the inside. He's afraid of rejection, but so am I.

What if I'm asking too much? Maybe I've been reading the signals all wrong. But the way he's looking at me now, I don't think so.

"What else do you want for your birthday, my darling?"

*Darling. He called me darling.* In that sexy British accent too.

All of my worries melt away and it takes my last drop of self-control to not swoon.

I finally rest my hands on his chest. Sure enough, the quick thump-thump of his heart-beat is pounding against my palms. I press my body against his and I'm flooded with heat.

"Will you consider breaking the terms of our contract?" I ask, not breaking eye contact. Sebastian hesitantly rests his hands on my exposed back, and his fingers graze my skin in the most delicious way. Every part of me is on fire now.

I stare him down, daring him to deny my request. A slight pool of sweat has collected on his brow, but he doesn't look nervous. He puts more pressure on my back with his hands and drags the material of my dress over my shoulders, letting it fall to my elbows. The only thing holding my dress up now is the fact that my hands are still on his chest.

He leans down to kiss me on the sensitive part of my neck and I let my head fall back with a groan. He traces little circles over my arms with his fingertips. When he finds his way to my neck, he takes a fistful of my hair and tugs on it. I feel him smirk at my responding moan between kisses.

Being touched and kissed like this is setting me alight with need. Before I know it, I'm listing all the reasons why it's okay.

1. Legally, we're married.
2. It's glaringly obvious that there's chemistry between us.
3. The past two weeks have been a total dream.

I fail to come up with a single reason why this isn't the right thing to do.

Maybe we can rip up the contract and stay married?

But then Sebastian's mouth finds mine and I stop thinking altogether. Now is not the time for deep thinking. Now is the time for action.

"Tell me what you want," he murmurs against my lips. "I need to hear you say it."

I arch my back as his hands roam down and rest on my hips. "I want you."

No. I *need* him. Not want. The blazing need inside of me is all-consuming now.

There's been an emptiness I've never been able to fill. And the yearning to be with this man, to cross that line and succumb to my every desire with him, is too much to resist.

"You want me... To do what?" he asks.

A moan rips out of my mouth as he leaves a burning trail of kisses down my neck and to my collarbone. He's taunting me. This is torture. Why won't he just get on with it and do as I ask? Do I really have to be more obvious?

I suck in a breath and force my brain to string a sentence together. "The night of the party, you told me there were things you wanted to do to me. Remember that?" I can barely get the words out, my voice rising in pitch as Sebastian's lips heat up my skin.

He lifts his head to look at me and a wicked grin takes over his face. "Yes."

I nod. Sweat is gathering at my hairline and our breaths are hot and rapid now. I yank on the collar of his shirt and give him a hard look, daring him to deny me a second longer. "Show me what you want to do to me. Now."

Sebastian lets out an agonized groan and his body vibrates against mine, then he walks me back to the bed, his hands squeezing my hips on the way over. "With pleasure," he growls.

# SEBASTIAN

*P*eyton is a goddess. The next morning, I lie awake watching her sleep as weak morning sunlight settles on her pretty face. I haven't slept a wink, too worried that if I fall asleep, I'll wake up alone in my own bed and find out that this was all a dream.

Her dainty hand is resting on my bare chest and I daren't move, for fear of waking her up. She looks so peaceful, so content. She must be dreaming, because every now and again she giggles softly.

I wonder what she's dreaming about, and hope I get to see her like this for many more mornings to come.

Her lips are red raw and the razor burn along her jawline tells me I should shave before the next time we do this.

My stomach tightens. *Next time.* I like the sound of that.

Lying in bed with her feels as normal as breathing. And now that I've found my equilibrium, it's going to be impossible to rest in a bed without her beside me ever again.

Peyton stirs and I smooth her hair, trying to stroke her back to sleep again. I'm not ready for the new day to come. After all the meetings I rescheduled, today is set to be manic.

All I want to do is call in sick and stay in bed with Peyton. My wife.

Last night, we broke all the rules. I may as well rip up the contract altogether. And would that a bad idea? I'm not sure.

The plan was to unlock my inheritance, not to fall for anyone.

But as I watch Peyton sleep, her bare skin kissing mine, I can't deny the fact that I've fallen hard for her.

She's all I want. If the solicitor got back to me and said that I'd lose my inheritance if I stayed with her, I wouldn't care.

If I lose my business, the house, everything I've built, I'd still be happy. As long as I have this woman in my arms.

Suddenly, a pair of brown eyes blink at me and my mouth tugs up into a grin. "Good morning, darling."

Her eyes light up at my greeting.

She pulls the sheets up to cover herself and blushes. I wrap my arm around her. "Don't do that," I say. "I like seeing you this way."

"And what do I look like?" she asks. Her voice is still heavy with sleep. She rests her head on the pillow and draws patterns on my chest with her finger. I cast my eye over her soft curves. Her tangled hair is splayed out over her back and her mascara is smudged around the creases in her eyes. "Undone," I say, settling on the best words to describe her. "Free. Exquisite."

Peyton bites against a grin and buries her face in a pillow. The next thing I hear is a muffled squeal.

The next time I hear her voice, it's coming from across the room.

"Oh my gosh. Yes, Sebastian."

Peyton's head snaps up and we both stare

at the birdcage in horror. Larry is looking at us
with one beady eye, ruffling his feathers.

"Did he just say…?" Peyton begins. The
bird opens his beak again.

"Yes, Sebastian. Yes!"

Peyton and I look at each other, then she
bursts into laughter. Last night, I was so
focused on worshipping Peyton's body; I didn't
notice the nosy bird sitting in the corner.
Good grief. He was watching us the whole
time.

"Why didn't you put him in the aviary?" I
ask her.

When she's done laughing, Peyton sits up
and the sheet falls. Now I've completely
forgotten what's so funny.

"Because Larry likes being in my room.
And I was lonely."

Ah. That comment grips my heart in a
vice. She was so lonely she smuggled a bird
into her room to keep her company.

But before I can think of a reply, my
phone starts to vibrate. It's on the floor somewhere. I roll out of bed and rummage around
in my pants.

"What time is it?" Peyton asks. She sounds
panicked. I reject the call and turn back to my

naked wife, who is now scrambling to make herself a toga with the sheet. The sunlight is making the material so sheer, she needn't have bothered to wrap herself up in it.

"It's time to get ready for work." I stand up and walk around the bed with a swagger to kiss my gorgeous wife on the cheek. "I'm going to take a shower. Would you like to join me?"

Peyton giggles as I give her a light tap on the butt. My phone starts to vibrate again and we both groan.

"It's Lloyd's agent," I tell her. "He's going to keep calling until I pick up. Will you take the call for me and tell him not to worry? I'll be there for the eight o' clock meeting."

Peyton nods and I flash her a cheeky grin as I leave the room.

When I return, dressed in my Gucci suit, Peyton is rushing to put on a pair of gold knotted earrings and simultaneously stepping into a pair of slingback heels.

"Are you ready to go?" I ask, offering my arm. Peyton grins, straightens out her pant legs and shrugs on a black jacket. Then she takes my arm and squeezes my bicep as we walk out into the hall. "Oh, by the way…"

She halts and looks at me with bright eyes. I steal another kiss before she can finish. She giggles again.

"That wasn't the agent," she says, handing me my smartphone. "It was your dad. He said he's in town tonight, so I've arranged for us all to go out to dinner."

The words rings like the belles of Notre Dame and my heart stops dead in its tracks.

"What did you just say?" I ask in an acid whisper.

# PEYTON

This morning, I was the happiest I've been in my entire life.

Apart from waking up with aches in places I didn't know could ache, I figured nothing could wipe the smile on my face. Especially after seeing Sebastian strut around the room in nothing but his Calvin Kleins. That view is enough to make any day a good one.

But as soon as I told him about dinner with his dad, something was off.

I click on my pen incessantly during lunch, staring at the computer screen and trying to look like I'm working out Sebastian's complicated schedule for the week. In reality, I'm trying to work out why Sebastian's face paled at the mention of his dad.

He didn't say anything after I repeated the facts. His dad and stepmom just flew in from Australia and will be in the city tonight. I made reservations at his favorite Italian restaurant.

But the way he looked at me, I might as well have told him that World War III just started, with a nuclear missile headed straight for New York.

When I saw his reaction, I wanted to talk to him about it, but Sebastian went right into boss mode and buried himself in work. And that wasn't hard to do at all, seeing as he pushed all of yesterday's appointments to today.

I sit at my desk and cast side-glances at his office. He's been having meeting after meeting. In the meantime, my stomach is a swirling mess of writhing snakes. The rising nausea gets worse as the end of the day approaches.

When we finally return to the car, Sebastian's jaw is jutting out and he won't look at me. "Do you want me to cancel tonight?" I ask him, trying to make eye contact as we arrive at the house.

Sebastian switches off the ignition and shakes his head. "We have to go now. I just wish you consulted with me first, before making plans."

I want to make a point that it's his dad. He's in town. How is this something we need to discuss? Surely, it's safe to assume he'd want to sit down and have dinner with the man.

I wonder if he's upset that I spoke to him and told him I'm Sebastian's wife.

But there's no time to speculate on Sebastian's mood change. We go our separate ways, get ready for dinner in top speed and reunite in the entryway, dressed up like we're going to the opera.

I chose a long, red gown with a ruffled hemline and a pair of black satin gloves that come up to my elbows. With my dark hair twisted up into a high bun, I feel like a million dollars.

I'm disappointed when Sebastian's gaze only takes in my appearance for a splinter of a second before he mutters, "Come on," and strides out of the house.

I can't say I'm not a little hurt by that.

Sebastian's parents are already seated when we arrive at the restaurant. I see the resemblance between father and son immedi-ately. The only difference is Sebastian's dad is sporting a few lines near his eyes and some silver streaks of hair near his ears.

"Sebastian, my boy. Good to see you. Good to see you."

Sebastian lets his dad slap him on the back and nods his head. "Hello father."

The tension in Sebastian's voice is impos-sible to ignore. But his dad's charismatic smile remains firmly in place as though he isn't picking up on his son's body language.

"So, this is the lovely Peyton," Sebastian's dad announces once his gray eyes land on me. He opens his arms and I walk in for a hug. "I'm Walt. We spoke on the phone this morning."

"Well then, I guess I should call you dad," I say and we both share a smile. A blonde-haired woman who can hardly be two years older than me breaks into a high-pitched laugh for no apparent reason. Walt gestures to her like she's a prized trophy. "This is Betty. She's my sexy minx."

"Oh, Walt. Stop it, I'm blushing!" She's not blushing at all, actually. She pulls me and

Sebastian in for a group hug and clutches my arm in an iron grip with bony fingers.

We settle down for dinner and Sebastian barely lifts his eyes from his plate. I'm left alone to try and answer the barrage of questions they fire in our direction.

*How did you meet? When did you fall in love? What was the wedding like? Why weren't we invited? Are you going to have kids soon?*

The list is endless, and I ramble answers to the best of my ability.

But the questions keep coming, and my irritation grows. I nudge Sebastian's arm, wondering why he won't even look up.

He finally opens his mouth.

"Are we going to get to the real reason you're here, or are you going to keep pretending we're happy families?" Great. He just made the situation a million times worse.

There's a beat of silence at the table, and Walt's gray eyes flash with annoyance for a second before he breaks into a polite laugh.

"Can't a father come and see his only son and his new daughter-in-law without scrutiny?" he asks, picking up his glass.

Sebastian lifts his eyes and gives his dad the coldest stare I've ever seen. And I've worked with the man for ten years, so that's saying something.

The bulge in his jaw is a big tell. I'm almost fascinated by how terribly this night is going.

"I don't have time for your charades. Either get to the real question you have for me, or be done with it."

Walt takes a swig of his drink and exchanges looks with Betty for a moment. He looks offended now, but unlike Sebastian, he's keeping his smile.

"Come on now, is there any need for this?" Betty begins. "We're all having such a lovely dinner. It'd be a shame to ruin it…" Betty begins, but she stops when Sebastian turns his cold stare to her. He shakes his head suddenly and pulls out a pen and checkbook from his jacket pocket. "How much is it?" he asks. The look on his face is almost daring his father to argue.

His dad opens and closes his mouth soundlessly, then chooses to take another swig of his drink. "We don't want money, I make enough on my own," he says.

I pick up my drink. "Oh, what do you

do?" I ask in an attempt to steer the conversation away.

Walt's eyes land on me. His smile isn't quite reaching his eyes. "I'm a cryptocurrency investor."

Sebastian snorts. His dad ignores it. "I help people mine crypto and sell them on the market." Then he talks at length about the fourteen hundred people he single-handedly turned into millionaires using his refined system.

Betty is all smiles as she nods along and eats her food. Sebastian let's out a derisive laugh. Then he signs a check and rips it off.

"Here, it's blank. I'll let you fill in the amount." He hands it over to his dad, who hesitates for a split second, but then takes the check and studies it.

"You really think I'm only here for money?" he asks, sounding like a broken man now. My heart contracts at the sight of his crestfallen face.

Sebastian pushes back his chair and rises to a stand. "Well, after thirty-eight years of experience, I find it difficult to believe otherwise. You're certainly not here to play the doting father, when we both know you've never cared about anyone other than yourself. Excuse me, I'm done." He turns to me and his eyes are blazing with fury. "I'm going home. Would you like to join me or continue this ridiculous dinner?"

I frown, not understanding what's going on. Should I stay or go? Sebastian sees my hesitation and nods with finality. "All right. I'll see you later then."

Then he marches out of the restaurant, but not before handing a server a stack of cash and whispering in her ear.

Once he's gone, I look at Walt and Betty in shock. "I'm so sorry," I say, picking up my drink again. "I don't know what's got into him."

Walt tucks the blank check into his pocket and his thin lips curve into a polite smile.

"No, *I'm* sorry. Ever since Sebastian lost his mother, he's had a chip on his shoulder. The man knows how to hold a grudge, I'll give him that." He glances at the door Sebastian walked through moments ago. "I just hope that one day, he will look at me again. Without disdain and judgement." His eyes grow misty. Seeing Sebastian's dad looking so wistful makes me jump into action.

"Let me go talk to him."

Before they can argue, I hurry after Sebastian and brace myself against the gust of wind outside.

Sebastian is still in sight. I run up to him as he walks along the street and grab his shoulder to look at him. "What on earth was that?" I ask him. Sebastian turns to me with a blank look on his face.

"Tell me, Peyton. How long have we known each other?"

I pause and look away to think about the question. "We're coming up on eleven years now…"

Sebastian crosses his arms with a hum. "And approximately how many times have I mentioned my father to you?"

My body is starting to feel like it's been dipped in an ice-cold bath. "Zero."

Sebastian cocks his head to the side. "So, why on God's green Earth, did you suppose I'd like to have dinner with him?"

Jarred by his question, I redirect with logic and reasoning. "Because he's your dad. Nothing changes that. If I could go back in time and talk to my birth dad, I would." I swallow hard as tears prickle my eyes. "I would give my right kidney to have *one* dinner with him."

Sebastian's expression softens for the briefest moment, but then he shakes his head. "You're making assumptions. I'm not you. My father is…" he grits his teeth and looks away. "You should have talked to me about this before you went making reservations."

I cross my arms. "And you shouldn't have stormed out of that restaurant like some moody teenager. I mean, you're nearly forty years old and you behaved like…"

"Listen to me," Sebastian says abruptly. He drops his arms and leans in. "I have my reasons. And if you want to talk about this, we can. At home. But I am *not* playing my father's silly games. And I am most certainly *not* having this conversation out in the street. So, let's go home and I'll tell you everything." He lifts an expectant brow, but my frown deepens.

"I'm not just walking out on your parents like this. It's rude. They flew all the way down here from Australia to see us. And you think it's appropriate to just…"

"They got what they came for," Sebastian says, straightening his back and looking down his nose at me. "They're not here to exchange pleasantries. Trust me."

I shake my head, unable to believe what Sebastian is saying. I can't shake the icky feeling I have about all of this.

"I'm not leaving."

Sebastian shrugs. "Fine. Then I'll see you at home."

And he walks off.

I take deep breaths. My hands are trembling when I head back into the restaurant. Walt and Betty have their backs to me as I approach. When I get within earshot of their conversation, my ears prick up. I side step to a fish tank and pretend to watch the exotic fish swimming around while I listen to their conversation.

"How much are you going to write on it, babe?" Betty asks. Her voice is full of anticipation. Walt leans in to Betty and swirls the drink in his hand.

"Whatever you want, my dear. I told you he'd come good. He always does."

Betty giggles like a high-schooler who just got a credit card. "Maybe we can go back to the Maldives. We haven't been there since Elise…"

"Don't say her name," Walt snaps. I almost giggle. He sounded so much like Sebastian just then.

"Sorry, babe. It's just, back then, those steamy summer nights at the holiday resort while your wife had no idea…"

Walt's soft laughter lands on my ears like a hammer. "You want to recreate some memories, eh? Well, I'm sure that can be arranged."

Furious and unable to listen any longer, I step out and walk round to stare at them. Walt and Betty meet me with identical looks - two deer caught in headlights.

I wonder if my expression is as cold and sharp as Sebastian's. I hope it is.

"So, this is why Sebastian will hardly talk about you…" I say, balling my hands into tight fists. "You were having an affair. And you really are only here for money."

Walt lifts a hand and starts to speak but I cut him off. "I'm sorry. This has been a monumental mistake."

Walt and Betty both start to speak at the same time, but I ignore their voices and head for the door, every atom in my body trembling in anger.

*I* find Sebastian in his study, poring over a manuscript with a half-diminished bottle of wine on the desk. He looks up as I walk into the room. His eyelids are half closed. "If you've come to tell me to make amends with him, then you're…"

"No," I interrupt. I pick up the bottle and take a swig. "I've come to apologize."

I hold out a packet as a peace offering and Sebastian eyes it with suspicion.

"What's this?" he asks.

The corner of my mouth tugs up into a smirk. "Open it and you'll find out."

Sebastian takes the packet and opens it up. It's a dodo model. "What's this?" he asks again, but his face is already breaking into an amused grin.

I toss my hair back and perch on the edge of his desk. "I've behaved like a dodo. As soon as I realized you weren't happy about meeting your parents, I should have cancelled and heard you out."

Sebastian stares at the model and turns it over in his hands with a thoughtful hum.

"You got me a goofy gift." It's not a question. The corners of his mouth are twitching. I'm taking that as a good sign.

"I went back inside and overheard them talking. You were right. There was only one reason why they came."

I brush Sebastian's hair away from his forehead and he lifts his eyes to meet mine. There's nothing but warmth in his expression now. I cock my head to the side.

"I'm so sorry about your mom, and about what your dad has put you through."

Sebastian takes my hand and kisses it. Then he shuts his eyes for a long moment.

"You didn't know," he says softly. Then he kisses my hand again. "How can I be mad when I never told you..."

He stands and pulls me in for a hug. I clutch his back as hot tears threaten to fall. "I love the dodo and I appreciate the apology," Sebastian mutters into my hair as he rubs my back. "I will cherish it for the rest of my life."

I chuckle against his chest.

And just like that, all is right in the world again. We hold each other for a long time.

Then Sebastian kisses the top of my head and pulls back to look in my eyes.

"This is painful to say, but you need to know," he murmurs. I nod silently, holding my breath as he musters the courage to tell me whatever is going on in his head.

"My dad didn't want me. When I came along, I was nothing more than an inconvenience to him. So, he sent me off to boarding school as soon as I was old enough."

I place my hand on his cheek and I'm about to speak, but Sebastian isn't finished. There's a far-off look in his eyes as though he's replaying the memories in his mind's eye.

"My mom came from a wealthy family. My grandpa was an inventor, you see. He paid for my schooling, took me during the summer, and taught me everything I know about being a man."

His eyes darken with grief, and even though he's never mentioned his grandfather, the devastation on his face tells me everything I need to know.

He's grieving. How did I not see it before? All this time, I thought he was just having mood swings. Shutting people out for his own protection.

But there was so much more to it.

"When did he pass?" I ask. I try to keep

my voice soft, but the question stings him all the same. He almost winces as he meets my gaze. "Not long after New Year."

I suck in a breath. So recent.

No wonder he's been all over the place mentally. I sigh. "When my foster parents died, it took me years to get over it." I shake my head. "I don't think I'm over it still. But my most complicated grief is toward my birth parents."

Sebastian tucks my hair behind my ear and studies my eyes. "What happened?"

I rest a hand on his shoulder, willing the strength to open up. I've not talked about this to anyone. Reliving it conjures up painful memories. I look away.

"They were young when they had me. My dad was in jail for drug dealing. And my mom… Well, I guess she thought I'd be better off without her."

I pull in a shaky breath. "It took years, but I finally found them after my foster parents died. I was too late though. They were both gone. I was stuck grieving for a set of dead-beat parents who never wanted me."

I let him look into my eyes again and tears start to roll down my cheeks. Sebastian wipes them away and presses his warm lips to my temples. "I know it's hard to understand, but I will never forgive my father," he says.

I take his hand and hold it to my cheek. "When I went back inside after you left... There's something else I heard while your dad and your stepmom were talking..."

I don't have the heart to relay what I heard, but Sebastian's knowing look tells me I don't have to. I revert the conversation back to me to end his suffering. "I guess the biggest struggle I have, is wondering what's wrong with me? Why didn't my parents want me?"

"There's nothing wrong with you," Sebastian says, frankly. I give him a dark laugh.

"Sure," I say, sarcastic. "There's a lot of imperfect parts of my body to prove you're wrong about that."

I guess he's done talking because he silences me with a deep kiss.

The feeling of his lips on mine is like a healing balm to my troubled soul. He must feel the same because his kisses become more aggressive.

He undresses me right there and then.

"Stand in front of the mirror," he demands.

I do as he says and he stands behind me, his eyes dark and wanting. "Now tell me about all the imperfect parts of your body."

I hitch a breath and give him a confused look. "Why?"

Then I glance at the red stripes on my hips. His eyes follow my gaze and soon, his fingertips are tracing them. "Because, my darling…" he pulls my hair away from my shoulder and presses his lips to my neck. "There's not a single part of your body that I do not adore. And I'm going to kiss you in all those places until you adore them too."

Before long, we're lying in each other's arms, sweaty and panting. Our souls are now entwined in ways I could never imagine.

Sebastian starts to plant kisses all over my face. Then he gives me the biggest grin.

"How soon do you think we could book some time off?"

I stare at him like he just said the Earth is flat. Sebastian Rockwood never books time off.

"Well, we have the Elmer's launch in five weeks, then there's the audit a week after that… I think I could arrange something in a couple of months," I say, thinking about the long list of work planned.

Sebastian plants another kiss on my cheek and cups my face, grinning from ear to ear.

"Great. You know what I'm going to do?"

I turn to look at him. "What?"

His eyes light up. "I'm going to book our honeymoon."

# SEBASTIAN

The past two months have passed like a dream.

I still work like a horse and keep up with the daily routine, but now I have Peyton falling asleep in my arms each night, and I've never slept so well in all my life.

We're leaving for our honeymoon in just a couple of hours and I glance over at Peyton, still asleep.

The end of our contracted marriage is fast approaching. With just a month left, my mind won't stop racing to the future.

It really doesn't look any different from where I am now. For the first time in my life, I am living a reality that I'm happy in.

I never planned to fall for Peyton. When I had her sign the contract, I worried about the idea that she wouldn't follow through. That we couldn't make it work.

I even pictured a scenario where she would fulfill all her commitments and then disappear a millionaire, never to be seen again.

But this. I glance at my gorgeous wife. Her chest is rising and falling so peacefully. Birds are chirping outside, and I marvel at how lucky I've become.

They say you can't have it all. But somehow, I think that I do.

It's me and Peyton against the world, and that's fine by me.

I pull out a velvet box from my pocket and open it up to reveal the platinum ring with its cluster of diamonds. An eternity ring.

I have everything planned out. We'll fly into Venice, check into one of the most expensive hotels, and spend three solid days inside our room. I'll worship Peyton's body and soul until she's one hundred percent convinced she's the most precious human being on this Earth.

Then I'll ask her to stay my wife. Seeing as

she's already married me, I can't exactly propose. But I'll rip up the contract and we'll throw it into the water while we ride a gondola.

For the rest of my life, I'll make her blueberry pancakes for breakfast. I'll take her dancing; maybe we'll learn the Tango. She'll fall fast asleep in my arms. And when she's sick, I'll devote myself to helping her get better.

My only regret is that we didn't do this ten years ago. I consider all of the memories we could have made if I'd dated her sooner. We have so much catching up to do.

I want to spend the rest of my life making her feel cherished. Adored.

She stirs and rubs her eyes with a yawn.

I stuff the ring back in my pocket and walk over to the bed to give her a kiss. "Good morning, beautiful."

"Do you ever sleep?" Peyton asks through a yawn. I climb into bed and wrap her up in my arms. "Of course," I say, then I bury my face in her hair and kiss the back of her neck. "But only as much as I need to survive. I don't want to miss a second with you."

Peyton rolls over to face me; her face is

brimming with joy. "We're going on our honeymoon today."

I take her hands in mine and look into her dancing eyes. "I know. Are you ready for another adventure?"

Peyton gives me a coy smile. "I'm not sure I'm ready to get out of bed just yet."

I lift my brows. "Is that so?"

I climb over her and prop myself up on my forearms with a devilish grin. "Well, I'm game for another adventure right here."

Peyton wriggles out from under me, laughing. "Let me just run to the bathroom first."

I watch her go in her cute satin pajamas. Then I fall onto my back and stretch out with one hand behind my head and the other on the box shape in my pocket.

I can't wait to tell Peyton I love her and I want her to be mine for good.

# PEYTON

*I*'m standing in the bathroom of our Venetian hotel room, staring at the home pregnancy test with trepidation. My hands are clammy; waiting for the result is making me nauseous.

I'm late.

Sebastian and I have been so wrapped up in each other. For the first time in my career, I totally lost track of the days and weeks. At first, I put the bloating down to the fact that I've been gaining weight all year. Then I put the nausea down to heartburn; I can't ever get away with eating donuts after three p.m.

But after we'd spent a few days in the hotel room, it suddenly occurred to me that I couldn't remember the last time I'd had my period.

I pick up the test to peer at it. A faint second line is appearing. My heart picks up speed and I angle the stick around in the sunlight, trying to see if it's really there or not. It's definitely there. The second line is getting clearer as the seconds tick by.

I put the test back on the sink when I'm finally staring at two pink lines, clear as daylight.

I'm pregnant.

I don't know why I'm surprised.

Sebastian hasn't given me a day off in the past month.

If it was possible, I would expect to be pregnant with one hundred babies at the rate we've been going.

My heart bubbles with excitement as I rub my little bloated belly.

I'm pregnant.

The word excites me, but another wave of nausea hits me and I dry heave in the sink. When I'm done retching, I stare at the test again, just in case I imagined the positive result.

I'm going to have a baby. I'm going to be a mom.

I honestly wondered if this day would ever come. I picture what life might be like, raising a baby with Sebastian.

I have mental images of him reclined in his armchair by the fire, a sleeping baby on his chest while he reads a manuscript.

Or hiking in the forest with a little boy on his shoulders.

I picture us walking barefoot on the sandy beaches of Los Angeles with a young girl holding our hands.

I squeal. We're going to be a family.

But then I remember the contract comes to an end next month. Sebastian hasn't brought up the topic at all recently. What if he doesn't want to stay with me after the year is up? He's not even brought up the immigration application for months, other than to state that there have been more delays.

But now we won't even need to worry about that interview. When it happens, we'll be ready. Sebastian and I have become a real couple. They can throw any question my way and I'm sure I'll be able to answer it.

Maybe that's why Sebastian isn't so concerned?

Anyway, the past couple of months have been a dream. Sebastian and I are so wrapped up in love, it's hard to believe things can get any better than this.

The two little pink lines tell me otherwise, though. It *can* be better and it *will* be.

Now, I just need to work out the best time to tell Sebastian.

*S*ebastian helps me into the gondola and then steps in beside me. The Venetian buildings are exquisite.

The sun teases me into a sweat almost immediately, but it's a glorious relief from the wet and rainy year we've had in New York.

I glance at Sebastian. He's been fidgeting nonstop, patting his pockets and shifting in his seat. Every now and again his chocolate brown eyes meet mine and he winks or offers a smile. Then he looks away again.

I'm caught up in my own head, trying to rehearse what I'm going to say to him.

This might be the best time to tell him he's going to be a dad. It's such a romantic setting.

I play out the words in my head. *Sebastian, I have something to tell you… I'm pregnant.*

I shake myself. No. That doesn't sound right.

*You're going to be a dad!*

Nope. That sounds wrong too.

*You know how much we've had sex over these past couple of months…*

Definitely not that one.

I'm a mess of nerves and my stomach is flipping. I want to lean over and throw up. I swallow all the extra saliva in my mouth instead and take steady breaths.

"So, Peyton…" Sebastian says. I wonder if I've gone pale.

"I have a question," I blurt before he can say anything else. Sebastian clears his throat and pats his jacket pocket. "Okay, go ahead."

I swallow again. "How do you feel about kids?" I ask.

Sebastian's thick brows rise so high; they disappear behind his hair. "Children? What about them?"

I fiddle with my bracelet and avert my eyes

now. "You know, being a parent. Having your own family... Having kids."

I glance up at Sebastian and notice his face has paled. "I'm not interested."

The words slice through my heart like a hot knife. "I'm sorry, what?"

Sebastian shrugs. "I'm coming up to forty. I have no desire to be raising kids at this stage of my life."

I sit there stunned, cradling my tiny belly as though to shield my peanut-sized baby from Sebastian's words.

"You really mean it?" I ask, frowning now. "You never thought to mention that to me?"

Sebastian looks at me puzzled, clearly clueless as to why my tone is sharp. "I thought it was obvious from the fact I've never talked about wanting to have kids, and we've been careful."

"Not careful enough," I mutter under my breath.

"What?" Sebastian asks, evidently not hearing me. I shake my head and force a smile.

"Forget it. You don't want kids. You've made that clear."

Sebastian frowns at me. "Is something wrong?" he asks.

Yes, something is wrong. Sebastian and I grew up with fathers that didn't want us, now I'm going to have a baby he doesn't want.

I shake my head. The last thing I need is for Sebastian to tell me to do something I'm not prepared to do. I'm having this baby. With or without him in my life.

The thought of losing Sebastian over this cuts me deep. I force a smile. "Actually," I say in an unnaturally high pitch. "I feel a bit seasick in this gondola thing." I look up at the man. "Can we go back now?"

Sebastian sighs heavily and rubs the back of his neck. I can't work out what he's so disappointed about. He's not the one who just got landed a bombshell.

*T*here's a tension in the air between us as we fly back to New York. When we get home, Sebastian is oddly polite. "Would you like to go to the spa today?"

My muscles are so tense from my stress; a massage sounds perfect.

When we get to the club though, we bump into the last person I'd expect to see.

"Mr. Martins," I call out. The oversized man turns and his eyes go wide when he sees me. "Mrs. Rockwood. Mr. Rockwood."

"Do you know what the holdup is with the application? We've not heard anything in months," I ask.

A tall man with a narrow nose pulls a face and claps his hand on Tony Martins' back. "Application?"

I look up at the man. I don't recognize him. He reaches out and offers me his hand. "Henry Wallace. I'm a friend of your husband."

I glance at Sebastian. He looks stiff as a board, but he's staring at Tony like he wishes he could shoot lasers out of his eyes. I turn back to Henry.

"Tony is our lawyer," I explain, offering a smile. To my surprise, Henry bursts out laughing. "You're pulling my leg. If Tony is a lawyer, then I'm the Queen of England."

Frowning, I look from Tony to Sebastian.

Both of them look extremely uncomfortable. "Sorry… but what did you just say?"

Tony breaks into an awkward laugh. There's nothing authentic about it. "Don't listen to my friend, he's British. Odd sense of humor. Very dry. Hard to understand, you see."

He looks like his collar is suffocating him. He tugs on it. "I'd love to stay and chat, but I have an appointment…" Then shuffles off at top speed. Meanwhile, Henry looks perplexed. Sebastian speaks up quickly.

"Sorry, Henry, but Peyton and I are late for a massage." He motions for me to follow him, but I lift my palm. "Hold up a second." I turn to Henry. "Are you saying that Mr. Tony Martins is *not* an immigration lawyer?"

Henry snorts. "You're joking, right? He's my accountant, and not a very good one at that. He's made a right mess of my books."

I look at Sebastian for an explanation, but he won't meet my eyes. Instead, he makes excuses to Henry and pulls on my hand. I let him lead me to a quiet seating area. Now alone, I yank my hand back and glare at Sebastian. "What's going on?" I demand, folding my arms.

Sebastian rakes a hand through his hair with a heavy sigh.

"All right. I should have told you months ago," he says. "But the longer I waited... The harder it's been to bring it up. So, I guess I just thought it would be best to... Not talk about it at all."

He won't look me in the eye.

"Sebastian. You're rambling," I say in my warning tone.

Finally, Sebastian looks at me. I mean, he really looks at me. His eyes are wide open and glistening. "I'm so sorry," he says, taking my hands. I stiffen, waiting for another bombshell to land. He takes a breath. "There is no immigration application."

I blink several times, too stunned to say anything. But Sebastian ploughs on. "I made it up. I got citizenship a couple of years back. Tony is just an accountant who likes to do improv."

My arms are going numb. "Improv?" I repeat.

I'm struggling to make sense of any of this.

"It's... A form of acting," Sebastian winces under my glare.

"I know what improv is," I snap. "What I don't understand is why you've gone to such length to lie to me about this. And if you don't need a visa, then you don't need to be married to me. So, what the *heck* was all this for?"

Sebastian's eyes dart rapidly, maybe searching for a part of my face that isn't angry. He looks frantic. He takes me to one of the empty couches and launches into a full explanation.

He tells me his grandfather left a multi-billion-dollar estate behind when he died, but it's in a trust until Sebastian celebrates his one-year wedding anniversary.

He didn't want to tell me about it, in case I turned into some gold-digger who wanted in on his inheritance.

So he came up with the immigration lie to pacify me.

When he's done talking, my blood is boiling.

"I can't believe you lied to me for so long," I say acidly. But the truth is, I'm not angry at him. I'm furious with myself for not reading the signs. I *knew* he was hiding something! My gut told me something was off.

"I'm so stupid!" I blurt, yanking my hands

away from him. "I wanted to believe you so badly, I ignored all the flags."

I stand up and start to pace. Sebastian looks up at me with devastation.

"You have every reason to be upset with me," he says, his voice low. "What can I do to fix this?"

I make a derisive laugh. "Nothing." Then I stop pacing and look at him with the most poisonous glare I can muster. "You can't fix this. Don't you understand? You've been able to hide something this big all this time without me knowing."

Sebastian looks down, his brows knitted together. "I'm sorry."

I place a protective hand over my stomach. "Sorry doesn't change the fact that you felt it was necessary to keep lying to me. If you can hide something this big for this long, how can I ever trust you? What else are you hiding from me, Sebastian?"

The words are like blades as they rip out of my throat. Tears prickle my eyes. Sebastian looks up at me. "I promise; I will tell you everything. I'll never hide anything from you again." He tries to take my hands but I pull away again, shaking my head.

"This isn't going work," I say mostly to myself.

"Please. You don't mean that," Sebastian says, his voice cracking.

I look at him again and my heart splinters in two. "Yes, I do."

He doesn't want kids. He's been lying to me all this time. It's just not a foundation for a healthy relationship. And I'll crawl over broken glass before I put my baby in that kind of situation. A liar for a father? Never.

I won't do it. My baby will grow up feeling loved. Supported. Wanted.

Hot tears flood my view of Sebastian. Then I clear my throat and muster all of the strength within me to say the hardest four words I've ever had to utter. "I want a divorce."

# SEBASTIAN

$\mathcal{I}$t's been a month since Peyton asked for a divorce. It's felt like somebody took me out of my body and I've been floating around like a soulless zombie.

I am numb.

Once the initial devastation faded, anger took over. I spent long hours at work and even longer hours at the gym pumping iron and taking out my frustration on the punching bag.

I was *so* close to telling Peyton I love her. So close. But that big-mouthed Henry had to go and spoil everything.

The truth is, Peyton is right. I've confessed it to myself many times in the past four weeks.

If I could successfully hide something that big for so long, of course she's going to wonder what else I haven't told her.

The way she looked at me though, one might have thought I have a secret family in Montana or something.

I pace my office clutching the divorce papers. I don't think I have the capacity to feel anything anymore.

Peyton moved back into her old apartment with Larry. The house has been eerily quiet ever since. I even miss the crazy parrot's squawks.

I feel lost.

My equilibrium is in shambles and I don't know how to function as a human being anymore. Not without Peyton.

Shortly after she moved out, she handed in her resignation and signed herself off sick. She won't see me. Or even pick up my calls. I only get the occasional letter from her divorce lawyer.

She's not asking for anything. Not even a cent.

And with the pre-nup already in place, the process is almost too slick.

I know the right thing to do is to give her what she wants; a quick divorce.

But every time I go to sign the papers, my hand trembles and I can't bring myself to do it.

I toss the papers on my desk and walk into my bedroom. If I were a religious man, I'd pray. There have been many recent moments in which I wished I *did* believe that there was a loving, omnipresent God out there who could wipe away all of my sins and change Peyton's mind.

But a memory comes back to me as I stare at my nightstand. I realize that even if there is a God, he's probably ashamed of me.

He's probably been disappointed in me for a long time. Ever since I said those things to my grandpa the last time I spoke to him.

I'll never be able to make that right. He's dead.

I shut my eyes as the thought stabs me in the chest for the first time in a while. He died before I could even apologize. How was I to know he was hiding an illness?

The man was like a lizard. He showed no weakness until whatever he was hiding took him.

If I'd known... If I'd had even a hint that he was going to be gone so soon... I would never have said those things.

With nowhere else to turn to, I go to my nightstand and pull out Grandpa's unopened letter from the drawer.

*Dear Sebastian.*

*If you are reading this, then sadly, I am no longer with you.*

*This saddens me for many reasons, but mainly because I know that you are most likely alone. My dear grandson, of whom I am so proud, my final wishes are that you stop putting walls up and shutting people out.*

*Yes, keeping people away will prevent hurt and suffering. But, my dear Sebastian, a soldier may stab himself so that his enemy cannot do it first, but in the end, he has caused his own destruction. How is this better than fighting?*

*I told you to find a wife. A mate. A friend. Someone to share experiences and all that life has to offer. It pains me to see you limiting yourself.*

*You deserve a happy, healthy life just as much as any other person. And so, my somewhat unconventional bequest regarding your inheritance is to ensure that you at least try to open up to someone.*

*I know that you will probably find a loophole or solution to this inconvenient problem I have presented you with. But after one year of marriage, one learns a lot about himself. You will be surprised.*

*I daresay that if you find a woman to marry, there will be ups and downs. There will be disagreements, apologies, forgiveness. A true love takes sacrifice. Even if the sacrifice is sometimes one's own happiness.*

*But therein lies the true meaning of love. I promise that if you try to let other people in, you will begin to see the world in technicolor. Or perhaps you might prefer to say high definition.*

*I apologize for my hand in our disagreement on New Year's Day. I did not mean to dictate or judge your life's choices. I only want you to be happy.*

*I hope that one day, you will find what you're looking for and that when it comes, you'll be filled with peace.*

*Do not grieve for me. I lived a mighty fine life. May yours be just as colorful.*

*Your Loving Grandpa.*

I look up from the tear-stained letter and take a deep breath. So, Grandpa expected that I'd try something unconventional to unlock my inheritance. In hindsight, I know that the argument we had was born out of his concern for me.

But at the time, I was too pig-headed to see it.

Sometimes, loving someone requires making hard decisions, I know that now. I think about Peyton - the agony of never seeing or touching her again. Never feeling her body in my arms. The pain floods me like a tsunami and leaks out of my eyes.

There is only one thing I can do to show her how much I love her. And no amount of apologies or gifts will change it.

I have to let her go.

# PEYTON

*I*t's been three months since I received the confirmation of my divorce. And now I'm sitting behind the reception of a small printing press, with a five-month-sized bump and a stack of debts in my name.

I rub my belly and the baby wriggles. The sensation makes me smile. The doctor tells me it's a girl in there. She's the reason for the little happiness I have left in my life.

I don't regret anything. All the sleepless nights of crying into my pillow, all the painful memories that taunt me while I'm awake... The throbbing ache in my chest that simply won't go away.

It's all worth it. Because soon, I'll have my baby girl. And she will have me.

We won't have much. I'll have to sell my plasma to buy her a bike. And I'll have to learn to sew all her Halloween costumes. But she will have all of my love. I can only hope that will be enough.

After another long, boring day, I climb out of the cab and walk up to my apartment, sorting through my keys.

A gasp makes me look up in alarm.

Sebastian is standing outside my apartment.

My brain can't process it fast enough before Sebastian rushes to me, his eyes wide at the sight of my bump. Then he collapses to his knees and tears start to pour down his face.

"Peyton, why didn't you tell me?" he asks in a voice drawn out in pain. He sounds like he did ten rounds with Tyson before Dwayne Johnson kicked him where it hurts.

I clutch my bump protectively, but Sebastian shuffles closer and wraps his arms around my legs. "I miss you. I miss you so much it physically hurts to breathe."

Hot tears roll down my face and drip onto

Sebastian's hair. "Don't do this. Please," I whisper, shaking my head.

Seeing him grovel is almost enough to soften my heart, but nothing has changed. He broke my trust.

"I'm sorry I didn't tell you about her," I say. Sebastian's head snaps back and he looks at me. "It's a girl?"

I swallow, willing every ounce of my energy to hold it together. I nod.

"I guess now we're even. We both hid things from each other."

Sebastian groans and pulls back to get a good look at my bump. "Please, can we talk about this? I can't bear being without you. I thought I could let you go. I thought it was what you wanted. But Peyton, you're having our baby…"

I press my finger to his lips and shake my head. "Don't," is all I can say. The pain is too much. I don't want to hear another syllable.

"I won't stop you from visiting. You can have as much contact with her as you want. But you have to go." I'm almost begging. The look on his face shatters my heart. He looks like he's barely slept these past few months.

And the hallow look in his face is more than I can bear to see.

Slowly, he composes himself and rises to a stand. His eyes never leave my bump.

"I had to try to win you back," he says. "I had to come and tell you that even though we're divorced, it's not what I want."

More tears leak from my eyes. "You don't want this." I point to my bump. "You made that very clear."

Sebastian screws up his face and shakes his head. "That's not fair. You didn't tell me you were pregnant, that changes everything."

"What does it change?" I ask.

Sebastian scratches the back of his neck with a sniff. "Well, when you're pregnant, it's no longer an idea. It's a reality. We're going to be parents. I don't want to be an absent father. I want to teach her to ride a bike. I want her to know that I'll beat up every guy who ever breaks her heart. And when she meets the right one, I want to be there to walk her down the aisle."

I pull in a shaky breath as fresh tears flood my vision. I blink them away and my heart swells as Sebastian talks. "I will remind her every day just how much I love her mother."

My breath hitches, and Sebastian takes my hands. "I know what I did was wrong. And I know I've hurt you more times than I can count. But if you'll let me, and I really hope you will let me, I will spend the rest of my life making it up to you."

I want to believe him. Every fiber of my being wants to believe that he's telling the truth. But there's something in me that just can't let go of the fear that one day, he might resent me. "You told me that your greatest fear is rejection," I whisper. Sebastian nods silently. I squeeze his hands. "It's because your dad rejected you, isn't it?"

Sebastian stiffens for a moment, but he gives me another nod. I glance up at the gray clouds above us and suck in another breath. "My greatest fear is to be abandoned. Because my parents abandoned me."

Sebastian searches my eyes. Then he pulls his hands from mine and cradles my face. "I won't ever let that happen again. I promise that our little girl will not be rejected and will not be abandoned. I swear on my life."

He leans in to kiss me but before he can, I whisper, "Those are just words."

He stops and lets me go. Then he blinks at

the ground several times with a slow, thoughtful nod. "I understand."

Slowly, he pulls out an envelope and hands it to me. "I'm moving back to England," he says and the statement hits me like a frying pan to the face. "I came to persuade you to come with me and start a new life together." His eyes look dull now. "I'll respect your wishes and keep a distance. But I will support you and our daughter. And I'll be back as much as I can be to visit with her. So long as that's all right with you, of course."

Hardly breathing, I nod.

Then with one final, sad smile, Sebastian plants a kiss on my cheek. "I guess, for now, this is goodbye."

I can't speak. So I nod silently and start to make my way up the steps to my apartment as little raindrops start to fall from the sky. It's as though the universe is weeping. I don't blame it. My heart is bleeding.

But then my foot slips on the step and I cry out as I lose my balance.

Luckily, Sebastian's big hands catch me and he wraps me up in his arms. I don't know if it's shock, pregnancy hormones, or the near-death experience, but I burst out into tears and bury my face in his chest as he holds me.

"I hate this," I say through sobs. Sebastian cradles me like I'm the most precious thing on earth and stays silent. "Why do you have to be so wonderful? And what is this anyway? Some love letter designed to make me take you back?" I thrust the envelope in his face. Sebastian chuckles and it's the sweetest sound I've heard for months.

"No. It's a check for one million dollars."

I gasp and lift my head to look at him. "But I broke the contract. Why would you do that? You didn't even know I was pregnant when you wrote that out."

Sebastian wipes my tears and his expression softens. "Because I love you, Peyton. I let you go because I love you. But I wanted you to have the money so you can find happiness. Even if it has to be with someone else."

That does it. The last fragments of my self-control fizzle away and I grab Sebastian's collar. "You're infuriating and impossible to stay mad at, do you know that?"

My voice comes out far too angry. I'm blaming the hormones for that, but Sebastian smiles. "If I asked you to marry me… again… Would you say yes?" he asks.

I hold my breath. Is he proposing? Three months after our divorce?

"If I marry you, will you promise to tell me the truth, the whole truth, and nothing but the truth?" I say, sounding like Judge Judy.

Sebastian's face is all sunny, even though the raindrops are heavier now.

"I swear."

"But you're frightened by this…" I gesture to my bump. Sebastian looks offended.

"I'm already in love with her."

"How?" I ask, blinking back.

Sebastian leans closer, his lips brushing mine. "Because she's coming from you. She's our baby. My heart is already wrapped around her tiny finger. She's going to get away with murder."

I laugh and look down.

Sebastian pulls back to study my eyes from a distance, as though he's looking for any uncertainty. "Peyton. Will you have me? The grumpy old boss you used to work for, who is irrevocably in love with you?"

His question is a healing balm over all the wounds I've been nursing. Now that I'm encased in his familiar scent, with his hands wrapped around my waist, I can't even remember why I was mad at him.

He loves me. He loves me so much he let me go, and still wanted me to have the million dollars so that I could find happiness without him.

Yet, the truth is, the only path to happiness is for us to be a family.

We can give our baby what neither of us had. My heart begins to race at the certainty that I love him too.

"Yes," I breathe. Happy tears flood my eyes. Sebastian's face lights up.

"Yes, what? I need to hear you say it," he demands.

I blink the tears away and pull him in for a kiss. When we break apart, I give him a sincere look. "Yes, I will marry you... again."

# EPILOGUE

## SEBASTIAN

Christmas lights are hanging on every tree in the garden, letting off vibrant multi-colored light. Once again, Peyton has outdone herself with the decorations. Tall candy canes are lined up on either side of the garden path, up to a stand with a chair set in the center.

Twenty-four three-year-olds are running around, hunting for reindeer cookies that Peyton has hidden. And Christmas carols are on full blast.

Parents are standing with their drinks, talking about Santa Claus, Christmas lists, and grumpy, overworked elves.

Peyton is among them, cradling her oversized bump in a long red gown with white trim. I love it. Her dark hair is pinned up at the back of her head and everyone keeps telling her that she's glowing.

It's true. She *is* glowing.

Her face is radiating happiness as she talks to all of her mom friends. Audrey runs up to her, our sweet little girl, her brown hair up in a ponytail. She's wearing a poufy white dress with a red satin sash at the waist. She turns around and asks her mother to tie the ribbon on the back. Peyton tries to stoop down, but her bump is in the way.

I chuckle and walk over. "Let me do it," I say softly. "You need to rest, darling."

Peyton laughs the comment off with the surrounding guests. "Sebastian worries too much. He forgets this isn't the first time I'm doing this." She pats her bump and sticks her tongue out at me.

I finish tying the bow on Audrey's dress and give her a soft kiss on the cheek. "Thank you, daddy," she says in her sweet voice. Then she's off again to join the other children.

I turn back to Peyton and place a hand on her bump. A soft kick protests my touch and I smirk. "You're growing a strong boy in there," I say, grinning.

Peyton chuckles back. "I know. He's been using my bladder like a punching bag. Do you hear me, little boy?" She pats her stomach while everyone laughs. "This is your eviction notice; I want you out before Christmas so we can give you all of your presents!"

Peyton is a natural mother. She's kind and caring, always thinking of ways to make Audrey's world a little brighter. The other mothers laugh about the little notes she leaves in Audrey's lunchbox, telling her that she's loved. But what they don't understand is that it's Peyton's way of healing from her past. She bears her scars so well, always covering them up with smiles and all the love in the world, so that our children never grow up thinking they aren't special.

I look out at the garden full of happy children. Two of them are standing outside the aviary, giggling as they listen to Larry the parrot chatter away.

My heart swells against my ribcage.

All this time, I was experiencing the world in black and white. That is, until I took a leap and let Peyton into my life.

I raise a glass to the heavens with my arm wrapped around my wife and nod.

*You were right, Grandpa, thank you for helping me to see in HD.*

THE END

A.N. Thank you so much for reading Peyton and Sebastian's story! If you enjoyed it, it would mean a lot if you would leave a nice review! And if you want more delicious boss romance, time to read Leila and Blaze's story in The Terrible Personal Shopper.

(Keep reading for a preview!)

# PREVIEW OF THE TERRIBLE
# PERSONAL SHOPPER

## *L*eila

"Leila Scott, you are, by far, the most incompetent staff I've ever had the displeasure of hiring. You're fired!"

The sous chef is currently looming over me in a cloud of garlic and ginger; his blood-shot eyes are bulging in fury.

I pinch myself.

*Dang.*

I'm awake.

This isn't my first rodeo. But no matter how many times it happens, getting fired hurts.

You'd think I'd be used to it by now – every job I've ever taken hasn't lasted more than a few months before I either willingly head out of the door, or my boss shows it to me.

Take my current situation for example. I've only been a waitress at the Perrier Francé for two weeks, and I just broke my third glass of the evening. Honestly? Those glass stems are just too thin. It's not like I'm the Incredible Hulk — my arms are as skinny as they come, and a lot of people tell me I have 'dainty' hands. I pretty much have the strength of a baby.

On second thought, that might not be the best comparison. I had a baby boy grip my finger that one time I worked in a daycare center, and no matter how hard I tried to prise his fingers open, the kid just wouldn't let go. Babies are crazy strong.

Anyway, I digress.

My first week at Perrier Francé, I dropped a couple of meals on the floor. But if I can just defend myself here; carrying three plates of food is hard. I mean, I only have two hands!

The sous chef didn't want to hear that, though. He demoted me to dishwashing duty in the kitchen, and that went fine, until I cut my hand on a steak knife. I didn't notice until

Ted, the health and safety guy, saw the pool of blood at my feet and started screaming about health code violations.

After that, the only things I was allowed to touch were wine glasses and glass cups.

But what can I say? Those things keep breaking.

I guess I'm small but mighty, and clearly destined for greater things than working in the back of a restaurant.

I pick up my jacket and trudge out into the alley with whatever is left of my pride, wondering what I'm going to do next.

A brisk, cool breeze whips at me as I trudge home, but the sparkling lights of New York City are warm and encouraging.

In this city that never sleeps, the night is young and so am I. I tilt my chin up at the skyscrapers and take a deep breath of smog and exhaust fumes. This is the land of hope and opportunity.

My purpose is waiting for me. I know it. I just have to discover it.

I follow the stream of people marching along and jabbering away on their phones or to each other. Everyone moves with intention here, like they all have somewhere very important to be.

I match their speed; it's either that or be trampled like Simba's dad in the Lion King. Plus, I *do* have somewhere important to go.

Somewhere *very* important.

I round the corner, look up, and grin at Elle's Kitchen. This is the one place I know I can get the best chocolate fudge squares I've *ever* tasted. Besides, Elle, who owns the bakery, is my go-to person in the city. She's a great listener, and she knows everyone, so my next job is probably going to come from her.

The bell above the door jingles as I push into the store. I look around at the many cake stands dotting the place. People are seated at small circular tables, talking about their day over a strawberry milkshake or an oversized cupcake.

Elle looks up from the counter. "Hey Leila! It's been a while," she says. Her blonde hair is pulled back into a high ponytail and her luscious locks are literally glowing under the LED lights in the store.

One thing about Elle is, her smile can light up a room. Right now, she's smiling at me like she doesn't have a care in the world, and suddenly, I'm grinning like I don't have any problems either.

I don't think anyone would be able to resist smiling back.

"Hi, Elle. Can I get three fudge squares, a vanilla cupcake, and maybe throw in a cinnamon bun just for good measure?" I position myself on a barstool by the counter while Elle hums and studies me with a thoughtful look. "Bad day?"

I rest my head on one hand and drum my fingernails on the counter with the other. "What gave me away?"

Elle shakes her head and her perfect blonde ponytail shimmers as it swooshes from side to side. She gathers up my order and I tap my card on the card reader as she slides my bag of comfort food to me. "Do you wanna talk about it?"

My shoulders sag and I heave a big sigh. "What's there to talk about? I can't keep a job if my life depended on it. My mom is ashamed of me, and if I didn't live with my sister, I'd have bailiffs at my door before the month is out."

Elle hums in acknowledgement and I know she has some pearls of wisdom to offer.

But another customer approaches the counter just then, and she turns to attend to them. I take the opportunity to pull out a fudge square and take a bite.

Usually, the taste of chocolate and gooey fudge is enough to turn any kind of day around. That isn't the case today. I swallow the piece and frown at the square, surprised that I didn't feel a rush or even an ounce of happiness.

"I'm so sorry," Elle says. I have her attention again now, and her eyes are full of sympathy.

I cringe. If there's one thing I hate more than getting fired, it's being pitied.

"I don't suppose you want me to cover maternity leave?" I ask, testing the waters. Elle steps back and fiddles with her apron. Her bump is even bigger than the last time I dropped by for a donut.

Elle clutches her bump and giggles "Maternity leave? I'm not taking one. Besides, Zane already hired staff to help out."

Zane Masters, the billionaire CEO of Got Cake? AKA Elle's husband. I've always found it odd that two owners of competing businesses got married. I mean, how did *that* happen? Word on the street is they were enemies. Now they're married and sealing the deal with a baby.

I sigh in defeat.

"Okay, it was worth a shot," I say, picking up my bag.

Elle is friendly and all, but I guess, with my track record, she wouldn't want to take a risk on me. But how hard can it be to serve customers at a bakery? The only thing I see going wrong is a waistline expansion after I've eaten more than my wage's worth of cake.

On second thought, not working at Elle's Kitchen might be for the best.

"Well, if you hear of any openings... You know, maybe some store manager crying about his lack of staff over a brownie..." I plop down from the barstool, and with a soft wave, leave the bakery.

I guess I was wrong. My next job isn't going to come that easily.

I follow the stream of pedestrians again, this time to the subway station, with my head down, and ride the subway train in thoughtful silence.

On a normal day, I'd look around and start talking to a stranger, or watch people. But the worry of where to find the next paycheck and how I'm going to break the news to my sisters is all-consuming.

I'm the oldest sister. I should be the example for them to follow - paving the way to health, happiness, and success. Without the good influence of our so-called parents, it's down to me to show the way. But I'm still figuring everything out, mostly with trial and error. And these days, error is the recurring result.

One thing I'm good at is acting calm. For the most part, I manage to hide my insecurities and clumsiness from my sisters. Around them, I'm a glass-half-full girl with a can-do attitude and the ability to turn any bad day into a great one.

To them, I'm Miss Silver Lining.

But on the inside, I'm an awful whirlwind of stress and worry. And that fact tends to present itself in particularly worrying ways. Like the time I closed a grocery store cash register with so much force, the dang thing fell off the counter with an almighty crash.

Or the time I tripped over my own feet while dog walking and dropped the leashes, setting six Great Danes free in the biggest park in New York.

Most people grow up to discover their talents or find their life's calling before they reach thirty. But here I am, months away from my thirtieth birthday, with no clue what I'm doing with my life. Where am I going? What do I want?

I know I don't want a big shot career. I'm not interested in wrestling with bureaucracy or spending the best portion of my life stressing over performance reviews and promotions.

No. Life is too short for that kind of stress.

I want to earn enough money to get my own place, and that's it.

Okay, maybe I'd also like to find a guy who can cook. Preferably, someone with the patience of a saint and the humor of a stand-up comedian...

Captivating eyes. Impressive cologne. Big, veiny arms. A heart-melting smile. Loves to clean. Respects his mom...

It's worrying how much the list grows each year.

I could totally settle down in the quiet suburbs with my shining knight, and then I can finally be a good role model for my sisters.

Instead of the total loser that I am now.

As I get off the subway and flag down a taxi, my phone vibrates in my pocket. All my thoughts scatter — which is definitely a relief, because I was starting to spiral into a dark place.

I pull out my phone, and my heart sings at the caller ID. "Josie! I'm so happy to hear from you."

It's true. Josie and I were roommates in college and I can't even remember the last time we spoke on the phone, let alone met in person. Soon after graduating in Fashion and Design, Josie reconnected with her high school boyfriend at a school reunion, married him, and started up her own business as a personal shopper.

She's the total opposite to me — refined, assertive, and has an eye for fashion.

Plus, she's totally successful in life, just ticking all the boxes.

Happy marriage – check

Great fulfilling job – check

A teddy bear-looking dog – check

Yep. The whole package. I half-expect this call to be the news that she's expecting twins.

That would probably be the cherry on the cake.

"Leila, I'm in trouble."

The first thought that crosses my mind is that it's a good thing I'm taking this call in a taxi. Five seconds earlier and I'd have been face down on the cold sidewalk, my heart hammering in my chest.

Josie is never in trouble. *Ever.*

"What's wrong?"

The panic in my voice must be obvious because Josie's tone shifts. "Oh gosh, no. Nothing's *wrong.*"

I exhale, my chest unhitching with relief. "Okay, so, what do you need?"

If nothing is wrong but she's in trouble, then Josie must be calling in a favor. And it's about time. I've lost count of the IOUs I've collected over the years.

"Right. So you know what I do for a living, right?"

I nod. I have a vague idea. "You buy clothes for rich people."

There's a pause and a light cough. I can picture Josie pursing her lips in an attempt to stop herself from correcting me.

"I help my clients update their closets,

yes." She says it like she's repeating what I said.

"Anyway, I've got an appointment in an hour at the Hilton in New York, and I'm stuck in Chicago."

I clamp my jaw. "You want me to cover for you?" I ask, my voice rising in pitch.

"It's just a meeting. There'll be no shopping or advising needed. I just need you to take my client's measurements, write down their likes and dislikes, and then hand them over to me."

I hum to myself as I think about it.

I wonder how many ways I can mess this up?

As I think it over, I can sense Josie getting nervous. She sucks in a deep breath. "I'll give you three hundred dollars if you do this for me."

I almost drop my phone. Instead, it flops from hand to hand, like I'm handling a fish. I grapple with it and then hold it to my ear again. *"Three hundred dollars?* Wow, Josie, you're really raking in the cash."

Three hundred dollars will help me find work. I might even get away with not telling my sisters that I lost my latest job. I can just tell them I left for a better one instead.

"Does this mean you'll do it?" Josie asks, sounding hopeful now.

There are butterflies in my stomach as I agree to it and end the call.

A few moments later, my phone pings with a last name, Hopkins, and a hotel address. Then I look down at my black pants and gray shirt.

*I can't go looking like this.*

Josie's clients are the cream of society. If I show up to a Hilton hotel the way I look right now, security will mistake me for a cleaner. Or worse, some kind of petty thief.

The taxi pulls up outside my sister's apartment and I storm in through the front door like a whirlwind.

Lucy jumps to her feet with a yelp and a game controller flies out of her hands.

"What's wrong?" she asks as I peel my clothes off and start to cover my body in a cloud of perfume.

Completely forgetting that I was going to lie to her, I tell Lucy everything at top speed as I get into my cutest outfit. Lucy just watches me, her eyes like two fried eggs.

"You got fired... Again?" she asks.

I ignore her while I grapple with false lashes for the first time this year. Lucy stands behind me, her big eyes unblinking in the mirror. "Aren't you worried about getting the measurements wrong?"

I chew my lip while Lucy takes the opportunity to list the infinite number of concerns that have magically come to life in her brain.

Everything from '*What if you need the bathroom during the meeting?*' to '*What if they ask what your opinion is on French designers? Do you know any?*'

Trust Lucy, the worry-wart, to flood my mind with all of her worst-case-scenarios.

What are middle sisters for, right?

Finally, she's done. I shrug and smooth my hair back into a plain bun. "Do you have a tape measure I can borrow?"

If I asked Chessy, our baby sister, the answer would be something like '*What the heck is a tape measure?*'

Chessy is a fashionista, but her delight is in the art of *buying* clothes. Not making them.

Lucy is my nerdy sister on the autism spectrum, with a passionate love of Lord of the Rings and cosplay.

Lucy beams at me like I just asked her to show me her Middle Earth memorabilia, then she disappears into her room.

I step into my black heels and look up to see Lucy has returned with a tape measure. She's holding it out like it's a Laurel wreath at the end of the Olympic Games in Ancient Greece. She drapes it across my shoulders and gives a little bow.

"Good luck," she says in a low and dramatic voice. I was a little nervous before, but now I feel like I'm about to take a gold ring to a fiery pit of doom.

I force a smile.

"See you later," I say. My wave a little too vigorous to be authentic. Lucy settles on the couch with her controller and puts her headset back on.

I let myself out and wobble down to the taxi waiting for me. "Take me to the Hilton in New York City, please," I tell the driver. Then I sit back and shut my eyes, trying to visualize myself not messing this up.

— Read the full story in The Terrible Personal Shopper, by Laura Burton.

# ACKNOWLEDGEMENTS

With special thanks to Vickie Betts (on TikTok) for coming up with the name Sebastian for me. You really helped breathe life into the character.

Thanks to Anne-Marie Meyer for her constant support and friendship while writing this book, she is a prolific and wonderful writer, if you enjoy my books you'll love hers too!

Many thanks to Ross, my real life prince who inspires all the book boyfriends I write about. For the patience, kindness and listening to me ramble, cry and rant about the process.

Special thanks to Tochi, my editor. Whom without, my books would be a rambled mess.

To Vanda, for not only being a fantastic proof reader, but someone I call a friend. Thank you for always being there.

And thank you to my agent, Bethany Weaver, for believing in my work.

And many thanks to you, my reader, who took the time to read this book and support me. I've been writing since I was a child, and making a living by doing what I love is a dream come true. Thank you for being a huge part of that.

Printed in Great Britain
by Amazon